Danger in Blackwater Swamp

By

Saundra Gerrell Kelley

SYP Publishing
www.syppublishing.com

Southern Yellow Pine
Publishing

Published by
Southern Yellow Pine (SYP) Publishing
4351 Natural Bridge Rd.
Tallahassee, FL 32305

www.syppublishing.com

Copyright: Saundra Gerrell Kelley 2013
Cover photo: Theresa H Gerrell
Author Photo: by Valerie Menard, Silentlightimages.com.
Cover Design: Taylor Nelson

ISBN-10: 0985706244

ISBN-13: 978-0-9857062-4-1

Printed in the United States of America
First Edition
May 2013

www.syppublishing.com

ACKNOWLEDGMENTS

My father, Ferd Gerrell, was born in Woodville near the St. Marks River in North Florida. While later he chose to live in Tallahassee, he never forgot his river roots. He passed his love of that place on to me and I love it with a passion that has never faded. Writing this book has only driven my roots deeper into that swampy soil.

I would like to thank my family for their support throughout the writing of this book. They served as reader/editors—Kitty Kelley Draa, Kristy Kelley, and Patsy Yawn were unfailing in their encouragement. My cousin, Philip Gerrell was a steady guide, helping me with scientific and archaeological terms; while Harry Shaefer and Bobbie Pell focused on the dastardly literary details I missed...I am indebted to all.

This book is also a salute to the work of Florida State University professor, the late Anne Rudloe, PhD. I took several of her naturalist courses at FSU. I enjoyed tramping around in the marshes and swamps learning from both she and her husband, Jack. Her work inspired some of the issues found in this book. The wild places of North Florida really are in danger.

Thanks also to Bobbie Ann Rice, a volunteer with Big Bend Hospice, for granting me permission to use her delightful name. For the rest, the names and characters are compilations of ones I grew up hearing. Some are from the numerous places I've lived; none are intended to be real persons. Some of the places, however, are very real, including the Goose Pasture, the Aucilla and the St. Marks Rivers, Dark Island, the sabal palm grove; the Riverside Restaurant, Posey's, and Myra Jeans.

This story came about when I spent the weekend with my aunt Margaret and Cousin Pam in Alabama. That night, a neighbor discovered a man digging around in the backyard. He kidnapped the woman and left her for dead in her own car far out in the country. A year or so later, I was telling a story in Lanark Village in Franklin County, Florida when a woman joined the circle. She told me about her aunt, who was murdered in South Alabama, and yes, it was the same crime! I knew then that I had the plot line for what I then called Southern Swamp Woman. I had toyed with it off and on for years while I finished my degree and pursued my career, but when I got the gist of the story, the characters took it away from me and ran straight through to the end. They became as real to me as my own family, and I could not stop until I brought them safely into harbor.

Saundra Gerrell Kelley

Chapter 1

BJ Hathaway woke early to the chimes in the tower of St. John's Episcopal Church across the street from the Floridan Hotel. She took a quick shower, packed her bags and prepared to leave town after the reading of Ben Taylor's will. The huge lobby, with its vaulted ceilings, painted open beams, suspended paddle fans, and oversized bamboo furniture beckoned, but there was no time to linger.

Soon after stepping through the arched doorway and into Tallahassee's heat, her thin white cotton shirt and linen pants clung damply to her body; heavy Navajo silver burned where it touched her skin. Irritated, she brushed back the wiry black and white tendrils that had worked loose from their French braid to curl around her face. Glancing at the old church in its shroud of moss-draped live oaks, BJ longed to enter the cool darkness of sanctuary, but there was no time.

Pushing through the early lunch crowd, thoughts of Ben's funeral the day before, and today's meeting, weighed heavy on her mind. She passed hordes of politicians with broad smiles and perfect teeth without seeing them. University students in T-shirts, shorts and flip-flops raced past her, and two elderly women, doddering along on their walkers, pulled aside to allow her passage. She was oblivious to them all.

Rafe Alford, Ben Taylor's best friend and attorney, scheduled the meeting immediately after the interment to allow BJ time to get back to New Mexico and her classes, which she appreciated. Something, however, niggled in the back of her mind as she trudged past the Chain of Parks and up the hill. It was a conversation she'd had with Ben some years ago. At that time, just as she was leaving to begin her career in the West, he reminded her she might need to return some day. She laughed then, replying, "I don't think North Florida can hold me, Ben, it's not big enough!" Somehow, she knew that comment would come back to haunt her, but not the way it happened.

1

A blast of cold air hit her when she opened the door to the attorney's office, jarring her back to the present. Miss Lydia Elizabeth Graham, Rafe Alford's long-time assistant, met her as she entered, saying, "Well, good mornin' Ms. Hathaway! It's been a long time since we saw you down here in Florida. I must say that I'm just as sorry as I can be about the reason for your visit. We'll all miss Mr. Ben."

Drawing her into the office, Miss Lydia continued, "Do come in out of that heat, ma'am," as she eyed BJ's damp shirt. "It has been monstrous hot down here this year. Now, would you like a Coke to cool you down?"

BJ nodded, "yes," and grinned at the term *coke*. Folk of the Deep South usually called all caffeinated sodas "coke", and she wondered what she would get. This time, however, the prim Miss Lydia gave her the real thing—an ice-cold Coca-Cola in a cool green glass bottle with a little white cocktail napkin to wrap around it. Drinking deeply, she felt the icy liquid slide down her throat, giving her system the jolt it needed.

That small ritual accomplished, Miss Lydia then ushered her into Alford's inner sanctum. Absorbed in the papers he held, Ben Taylor's attorney grunted when she entered, nodded to a seat, and continued reading. Wearing a lightweight summer suit, white hair brushed back and worn on the long side, he was an eccentric holdover from the old South. One who blithely ignored the fashion trends of the highly political town he lived and worked in.

"Where is everybody, Rafe? Am I the only one invited to this meeting?" BJ said as she sat near him, fanning herself. Restless and anxious for some reason, she rose and prowled his office like a svelte Florida panther. Deep windows with old, wavy glass overlooked a patio brim-full of red geraniums and white crepe myrtle in the shaded alleyway just outside, but it failed to hold her attention.

"Oh, come on, Rafe, quit ignoring me," she said, sitting down again. "I've got a plane to catch and you know it! What did Ben leave me, some of his favorite books and maybe the Bolen projectile points? I helped collect some of them, you know—or did he donate them to the museum?"

Finally, noting her obvious angst and need for haste, he lifted his eyes to hers, his face void of expression. Again, he glanced down at the document he held, and then looked at her over the top of his tortoise shell reading glasses without speaking. Finally, he cleared his throat and said, "No, BJ, I think you'll find there's a bit more to it than that."

Irritated, she crossed her long legs, swinging one sandaled foot impatiently and stared at the man, the slight crease between her eyes deepening. Glancing down at her watch, she tried again, "Look Rafe, I've got to get the car back by noon and my flight leaves at 1pm, so can we please get on with this?"

She was still calculating how much time she'd need to get to the airport for the first leg of her flight back to New Mexico when Alford's smooth voice intruded, "Just hold on to your shirt tails, Girl. You may be grown up, but you haven't changed one bit, have you? We're waitin' on somebody," he said as the phone rang, adding, "you always were the most impatient child I ever knew."

BJ's lips curled and her eyes crinkled at that. She was in her mid-fifties but she knew she would always be the child he knew in her youth to Rafe Alford.

Rafe listened to his assistant before continuing. "Okay, Lydia's got Matt Walker on the line—he'll be on speaker, since this reading involves him, too."

The mention of Matt Walker got her attention. She straightened up quickly, twisting the heavy silver ring on her middle finger. Then, with a distracted look on her face, she gripped the end of the long braid that ran down her back and held it like a talisman, waiting for the sound of Matt's voice.

Alford fumbled awkwardly with the phone, and then said, "Walker, you there?" The rumble that was Matt Walker's voice, answered him immediately. "You got me, Rafe, let's get on with it... and hello, BJ. Sorry we have to do this so soon after the funeral. I regret that I couldn't be there with you—we'll all miss Ben."

At the sound of the break in Walker's voice, BJ looked up quickly, murmured something in response, batted tears from her own eyes, and then stared into the alleyway.

Watching the girl-turned-woman, he had known for most of her life, Alford's eyebrows lifted imperceptibly, then he shrugged and got on

3

with the reading of Ben Taylor's Last Will and Testament. BJ found his slow, southern drawl agonizing in her grief and lust for speed.

"I, Benjamin Alford Taylor, being of sound mind and body at the time of this writing, bequeath to my goddaughter, Betsy Jane Hathaway, presently of Santa Fe, New Mexico, the bulk of my estate. My grandfather's muzzle-loader rifle, and the deed to the cabin adjacent to Taylor's Run, and leased from me by Matthew H. Walker, is to be transferred to his name at my demise.

All of my accounts are in order and will be at Ms. Hathaway's disposal when she chooses to make the river house her primary abode. It is my desire that she continue the restoration of the properties located in southern Leon, Wakulla, and Jefferson Counties began by me, and that at her demise, she shall insure its continued restoration and protection from development forever. My attorney, Rafe Alford, has drawn up the documents of continuance and a lifetime stipend is his as long as the two of you desire to work together on this project."

Benjamin Alford Taylor

Walker let out a loud whistle that pierced through the receiver and laughed, saying, "Well I'll be damned—he's left practically the whole thing to BJ. This news will upset paper company bigwigs and politicos from Tallahassee to Miami and back, that's for sure. Good for him!"

Suddenly, Walker paused, and then continued in a low voice, "And to leave me the cabin and his gun— I can't believe it!"

As Alford listened to Walker on the phone, he felt the stunned silence emanating from the woman sitting across from him, looked up and said, "Are you okay, BJ?"

He looked away after seeing BJ's face, allowing her the moment to digest what she had just heard.

BJ was silent, sitting with both feet on the floor, her body rooted to the chair, both hands gripping the smooth, carved arms, unable to breathe.

As Alford and Walker continued the conversation, discussing the details of Taylor's will, her mind wandered, not really hearing what they were saying. The beginnings of a headache provided a distracting backbeat to the chatter running wild in her subconscious mind. Ben had given her no indication he might leave his property to her. If she thought about it at all, it was with the assumption that his land and house would be turned over to a conservancy at his death. Now, as though speaking from the past he loved so much, he wanted *her* to finish what he had begun. The very thought collided with the grief she felt—it was unexpected and completely impossible, and she felt leaden from the weight of it.

When Walker hung up, Alford turned back to BJ, an expectant look on his face. "Well," he said, slowly and very deliberately, "What do you make of it, Miss Betsy Jane?"

That got her attention and she spit fire at him. "NOBODY calls me Betsy Jane, Rafe Alford, and you'd better not start now!"

He grinned at that and sat back, waiting for the tirade to subside. When it did, BJ was once again in control of her emotions.

"Are you sure about this, Rafe?" she said, a trifle embarrassed by her outburst. "Are you certain he was in his right mind when he wrote it? He never once mentioned it to me, and I can't believe he did this without consulting you."

5

"It's as real as we're sittin' here, BJ," he replied. Pausing a moment to choose his words carefully, he removed his glasses and continued, "Ben came in here a couple of weeks ago and gave me this letter. He basically told me what was in it, hired me to draw up the necessary documents of transfer, and then told me to get it notarized. We did everything that afternoon and Miss Graham notarized it for him on the spot. He took copies and told me to keep the originals in a safe place, which I did. It's like he knew his time was up and he wanted the will done his way with no interference. So yes, this document is legal and will stand up in court if it is challenged, which it won't be, I am sure. Ben Taylor never did anything half-way in his life. You know that. Do you think we could work together? Ben seemed to think so."

"Yes. Oh, of course—yes, we could work together, it's just that, well," BJ paused, stumbling over the words, "this is such a surprise. I'm not... I never dreamed...I've got to think about this Rafe."

BJ's voice faded away as she stood slowly, hugged the attorney, who was a distant cousin of Ben's, and turned to take her leave.

She stopped just inside his office, her hand on the cut glass doorknob and said, "By the way, when did Matt move down to the river? Ben never said anything about it to me."

"Well," said Alford, "He leased the cabin from Ben not long after you left. I drew up the papers for it. From what I understand, Matt was working in Florida a lot just then—you know, mastodons, and ancient manatee skeletons he found in some swamp muck—that kind of thing, so he made the place on the river his base of operations. He did a lot for Ben in these last years and they got to be good friends. They were close you know, almost as close as you were with Ben and Nora. Matt's a good man, BJ. Ben was careful who he trusted, and I think you can trust him, too."

"Oh, what about Jake Collins?" she added. "Have you heard anything about him lately?"

Rafe Alford chuckled deep in his throat, "Don't you worry about that bastard, BJ. He's safely locked away—we won't hear from him again."

Relieved, BJ nodded and promised to be in touch, then walked into the blinding light and smoldering, mid-day heat, fumbling in her purse for sunglasses. Just thinking about her childhood tormentor, Jake Collins made her aware of the headache again, this time throbbing in the back of her head. She wanted to cry, but there was no time to tend to her ragged emotional state. She had a car to return, a plane to catch and not much time to do it in.

* * *

The sudden loss of her mentor and trusted friend, and now, his strange bequest, played in her mind repeatedly like a stuck record, and she groaned when the headache roared back in like a freight train.

She couldn't get her mind off of Matt Walker either—it was like the proverbial itch she wanted to scratch, but was afraid of what would happen if she did. She wished for his sane, levelheaded presence so they could talk about this thing in person.

Barely into her thirties when they first met, BJ was newly divorced from her childhood sweetheart; the man she thought was her forever love. When Matt Walker marched into her life, the world rocked beneath her feet, leaving her exposed and vulnerable. Life as she knew it stood still for a time.

Ben frequently hosted parties for his archaeological colleagues at the house on the St. Marks River, and it was at one of those events they were introduced. As Ben Taylor's research assistant, she already knew about Matthew Walker, PhD, and was eager to meet him.

Ben gave her fair warning. "Walker's coming tonight, but you may have trouble getting to him BJ. Everybody wants a piece of him when he shows up at events," he said with mischief in his eyes.

She was excited about meeting someone of his stature in her field. Although he was only a few years older than she, his achievements in the world of archaeology were already legendary: he was part of the team that brought up the 16,000-year-old mastodon skeleton found by Buddy Hayes, a local diver, in the Aucilla River in 1968. Reassembled, the huge mammal was now on display at the Museum of Florida History in Tallahassee. He helped map a good portion of the Wakulla Springs cave system, had researched caves in the mountains of Appalachia, and was in demand as a speaker and author. However, when his eyes found hers, she forgot all of that. Instead, she found herself riveted in place by an immediate attraction that would not be denied. Nothing could have

7

prepared her for the excitement he generated in her that night, or the result of that attraction.

Tall, with iron gray hair that refused to stay put, clear, hazel eyes and a warm smile, he had a way of looking into her soul that she had never experienced before. She found the simple act of shaking hands with him caused electrical spasms that delighted and frightened her at the same time. She tried to ignore the attraction, but finally decided to embrace both emotions and enjoy the experience.

That night, they climbed the metal stairs up to the widow's walk on the roof to watch the stars reflected on the old river as it meandered out to the Gulf of Mexico. It seemed as though they had always known one another, and conversation was easy between them. They shared so much—a love of place and ancient cultures, books and music, animals and travel, and they talked through the night. By the time they descended the stairs and reentered the house, the guests were all gone and Ben was long asleep.

Hand in hand, they walked through the quiet house and down to her car. He kissed her then, under fading stars and a drifting moon—a kiss she returned in earnest and remembered always.

"When will I see you again," he said.

Fumbling in her purse, she gave him her card. "Call me," she responded with a tremulous smile. Shivering slightly in the early morning air, she drove away, watching him fade behind her as dull, sandy dust stirred in her wake. A brief premonition struck her then—whatever it was that had sprung to life between them couldn't last, but it *would* change her life.

Two years later, her fears were realized when their often fractious relationship ended. When the anger subsided, she knew the split, though difficult, had set her free to pursue her own dreams, a path she might not have taken had they remained close. She took a teaching position in New Mexico, attained the tenure track, and pursued knowledge of the cliff dwellers and their art.

Even though their paths diverged so sharply, both she and Walker followed one another's careers in academic journals and through their mutual mentor, Ben Taylor. On occasion, BJ acknowledged she still

8

missed the man who had come to be a part of her, losing sleep to the fire that simmered low in the pit of her stomach when she thought of him.

For some reason, Ben's decision to make them his sole heirs made sense and was appealing to her, in other ways it made no sense at all. She had made a life for herself in New Mexico, a life Ben encouraged her to pursue. She enjoyed the work and was good at both research and teaching, and her career had included the tenure track at the university. She made close friends and numerous contacts that gave her access to the culture she specialized in, the Pueblo dwellers. The thought of leaving it turned a wedge deep in her soul.

There was also always the concern of asthma, which had practically disappeared, in the hot, dry, western climate. Each time she returned to Florida, she brought out the inhaler and kept it nearby, just in case.

There were decisions she would need to make soon, and they were big ones, but her mind was in a muddle. She needed time to process Ben's death. Grief took time to heal and she would miss Ben for a long time. She'd miss the calls during the day or night when she could talk things out with the closest thing to a father she could remember. She now felt cut off and alone, but she also felt the need to escape the responsibility Ben was trying to get her to assume from the grave.

"What *was* Ben thinking?" she asked herself again. "I haven't even been home since his wife, Nora, died three years ago. I've built a career in New Mexico and have a good life of my own—what on earth made him think I would be willing to come back here to shoulder his dream and see it through?"

Still, something in Ben's proposal drew her back with memories of her old haunts. She felt like a migratory bird, or a butterfly finding the need to return to its place of birth, and yet, still, something in her resisted.

Instinctively she knew the answer to her questions and felt foolish for even thinking of it. Ben Taylor had always known her love of the place to be as deep as his, and in so doing, had groomed her carefully to assume the role of caretaker. What he did not want to do, apparently, was to limit her flight—her need to find herself, which she had done. Had he told her what he planned to do, she might never have left, but stayed to work at his side, never experiencing her own dreams of adventure and exploration. For that, she reminded herself, she was grateful.

There was no time to go down to the river house before she left. Truthfully, she really didn't want to see it just yet. She would have to come back after probate anyway, and Ben's death was too fresh and the memories of the old Florida house were too intense. Besides, there were classes to teach and appointments scheduled for Monday, and a flight to catch in two hours. She found her rental car and drove to Tallahassee's small airport, memorizing everything she saw. Again, she thought of Matt Walker, poignant memories of their time together completely intertwined with the place. Just being there and hearing his voice on the phone brought back a flood of remembrance. It amazed her that a man she had known intimately for only two years could still make such an impact on her.

* * *

Taylor's unexpected death after a car crash, the sudden trip to Florida for the funeral, and finally the reading of the will, left her little time to time to think, but the thoughts continued to intrude whether she asked them to or not. She was potentially the steward of a huge property far from her life out west, and she found the enormity of Ben's bequest overwhelming. She loved the coastal marshes and woodlands of North Florida. She knew them threatened in every way, but she also loved the southwestern Native American culture that was her principle field of study. BJ had learned to appreciate the hot, dry desert with its twisted trees, cactus, sudden rains, canyons and the Rocky Mountains, and the culture that evolved from it.

The more she thought about it, though, the more the idea of stewardship appealed to her. Maybe she could have both with careful planning. Even with Rafe's help, taking on management of the estate, and ongoing direction of the restoration was huge. Surely, by mid-summer she could make a decision about what to do with her inheritance and set everything in order.

Landing in Atlanta, she placed a call to Matt, finding the need to connect with the only other person named in Ben Taylor's will…or so she told herself.

"Matt, its BJ Hathaway, is this a good time to call?" she said, envisioning the tall man on the other end of the connection.

"BJ," he responded with warmth, and something in her relaxed at the sound of his voice, "I'm glad you called and no, there's never a bad time for you to call me," he said, and in his easy way, invited her to tell him what was on her mind. "Want to tell me about it?"

Briefly, they discussed the ramifications of the inheritance and in spite of her best intentions, BJ found herself telling him about her life out west and the conflict she felt about leaving it. There was little time to speak further on the issue—she had to board the plane, but she wanted to know where he was and what he was doing.

"I'm still in Miami helping to record the artifacts they've found near the big Native American circle," he said. "You know, the *Miami Circle*— it's located downtown on prime real estate, and has stopped a major construction project in its tracks. It's a major coup for the American Indians down here, and archaeology in Florida, too. That work is ongoing, but I'm working on what appears to be an additional ceremonial site nearby, and there's probably more buried underneath the buildings all around it. I wish you were here—I'd like your thoughts on it."

"Look, BJ," he said before she rang off, "You need to give yourself some time—Ben would expect you to do that. Nobody knew better than Ben what this would do to your life, but he also believed in you and knew you were up to the job. If you want, let me know if you decide to head back to Florida any time soon," he added. "My time with this project is almost finished…I'll make sure I'm home by then, okay?"

She agreed and closed the connection, smiling to herself as she thought about the conversation. After all their years apart, it appeared he was still the same man who wanted to know what was going on in her life, and still willing to listen when she needed to talk. She'd missed that unique aspect of being with Matt Walker, never finding it in subsequent relationships.

Distracted, she moved up in the queue with second thoughts about making contact with him again, "What have I done? I'm finally over that man and here, at the first sign of trouble, I've gone and called him like I was a school girl or something." She had to admit she felt

11

better for having spoken to him. After all, theirs was a strong connection through Ben, and now it would of necessity, if she accepted Ben's bequest, be even closer.

Still, they had not spoken in the twenty years since their relationship ended and she thought at the time she'd never see him again. Now, after hearing the sound of his voice, and sensing that old familiar warm feeling in her belly, she had to admit to a deep longing for Matt Walker that went beyond her dreams. What she didn't know was if she really wanted to encourage him again, or if he *could* be encouraged. Much had happened to both of them in the intervening years after their separation, but perhaps it was possible to begin again. It was also possible that her years as a single woman had taken a toll; perhaps she would find it difficult to let *anyone* get close again. It was also possible he had somebody else, but she pushed that thought out of her mind and boarded the plane.

* * *

After the call ended, Matt stared at his cellphone with a feeling of disquiet, then slipped it into his belt clip and tried to get back to work. He found himself distracted by the conversation with BJ and unable to concentrate for thoughts of their time together that intruded. Finally, he wrapped it up and went down to Juanita's Tamale Cafe alone, and wolfed down his supper with a shot of top shelf Tequila for good measure. A part of him satisfied, he took his time after dinner, strolling past Miami's glitzy department stores filled with luxury goods, listening to taxi cabs honking in the night and searching for the stars he knew to be overhead, muted by the city's lights. Camping at the site with several co-workers to protect it from irate developers and investors, he had managed to absorb some of the historicity of the area, and had come to appreciate its many contrasts. Considering all the archaeological sites he had studied, in Florida and elsewhere, this was easily the most novel: smack in the middle of colorful, loud, polyglot downtown Miami was an ancient circle of mysterious origin found prior to construction on a new building. He worked closely with the Native American advisers and the government, recording the findings and seeking to understand their significance. Now that they were almost finished, he found himself not only ready to leave the site, but also eager to see BJ. Whether it was the stirring of old affection, or the beginnings of a new friendship, he knew enough about BJ Hathaway to be very careful if she chose to move to the river. A wrong move might push her away again, and judging by the feelings she had aroused in him, he intended to be very careful this time around.

Thoroughly aroused, he thought of the tall, intelligent woman whose dark eyes, wild black hair, and high cheekbones had compelled him years earlier; his memories of her were very clear and disturbing. Sleep was long in coming.

When a flock of pink flamingos settled for the night in a shallow pool nearby, their wings a gentle whisper accompanied by a breeze in the Royal palms high above, Matt Walker finally slept.

Chapter 2

Picking up her car at the airport, BJ easily navigated Albuquerque, New Mexico's late Sunday afternoon traffic, and then drove out to her home on the edge of the desert. She took great pleasure in the drive to the outskirts of Santa Fe, delighting in evening's changing light. Martha, her black and white long-haired cat, was at the door when she walked in, meowing as though she had been gone forever instead of four days.

"Hey, little one, did you miss me?" she said. In answer, the cat turned away and ran to her dish with an expectant look in her eyes, fluffy tail straight up. "You are one spoiled cat" she said, but poured a bit of food into the bowl to placate the cat and felt better for leaving the cat behind. Mandy, the cat sitter, had done her job well, but Martha always let BJ know she was most unhappy when left without her mistress. After nibbling at a bribe of her favorite shrimp cat food, Martha jumped on the bed to help BJ unpack her bag. When it was empty she climbed into it, swishing her tail, meowing.

"Oh, come off it, cat," she said. "You've been petted and fed—I *know* this.

You will just have to get over it. Besides, we may be going on a long trip soon, so hang in there with me, okay?" The cat seemed to understand, jumped out of the bag and came over, rubbing against her legs. "That's much better, Martha, thank you!"

Later that night, when all was quiet, BJ heard the rusty sound of Matt Walker's voice in the back of her mind, and saw those startling clear hazel eyes—eyes that always seemed to look deep into her soul.

Distracted by the memories and the many decisions to be made, she called Analinda Perez—a fellow professor at the university, confirmed their carpool for 7 am the next morning, and reviewed her lesson plans. She then scooped the cat up in her arms, climbed into bed and fell into an exhausted, dreamless sleep. Martha, for once unresisting, seemed to understand BJ's need and stayed close throughout the night.

Waking at dawn, BJ stretched, got out of bed, and padded into the kitchen barefooted to make coffee, Martha at her heels. Vaguely disoriented, she peered out of the window and instead of seeing the green of Florida—the tall longleaf pine trees and spreading live oaks. She saw the umber desert spotted with cacti under a vivid blue sky, and tall, jagged mountains in the background. Something in her responded to the beauty, but there was also the ache for the familiar landscape of her birth, and it wouldn't go away.

Something settled in her mind during the night, and though she still felt conflicted, she no longer felt daunted by the prospect of the inheritance. Instead, she found herself looking around her comfortable home, thinking about what she should take and what to sell before moving back to Florida, and the possibility of keeping a small apartment in Santa Fe for continuing research trips. Life was full of possibilities and forked roads with many paths to choose from, but she was feeling better about this one after a good night's sleep.

Chapter 3

Morning in the desert was cool, dry, and invigorating when BJ stepped out of the house. She inhaled deeply, feeling strong and fit for anything that came her way. She drove the short distance to the car park, and joined Analinda and several other regulars—mostly faculty, for the carpool into Santa Fe. BJ told Analinda about her trip to Florida and the inheritance, Analinda's shock growing as she shared details.

"You've got to be kidding," said Analinda. "From what you've always told me, that place is a wilderness of tangled undergrowth, scraggly second-growth trees, and tourists. Just tell me this: what are you supposed to do with it, if you *do* decide to go down there? It sounds to me like you'd be leaving all you know and love to disappear into no-man's land. *Moreover,* what about the floods, hurricanes, and dangerous criminals running loose in that God-forsaken place? You hear all kinds of stuff like that happening in Florida. It's a place you're supposed to visit and leave—you know, fly into Orlando on a flight/car rental/hotel special, see the Mouse and some alligators and stuff, and fly out. You know that! Besides, everybody who lives there must be at least a hundred years old and shriveled up like old leather from too much sun."

BJ laughed at that, "As if we didn't have sun out here! No, it's not quite that bad. After all, Tallahassee *is* the state capital. It can be a bit of a backwater at times, but look where we are now! Besides that, my part of Florida still has some of its native ecology. There are even some pioneer-stock natives still living there with interesting stories to tell. It's *not* Disney World, you know. In fact, thank God, it's nothing like that, but there are folks who would like it to be, and I think that's what Ben was counting on me to prevent."

16

Analinda looked at her old friend with a frown on her face. "You're really thinking about doing it aren't you? You'd have to give up your life here, you know."

"Yea, I'm thinking about it. In fact, I'm seriously considering it," said BJ, a frown furrowing her brow. "I've been set to travel when I retire, not begin a new career! I haven't completely made up my mind what I want to do. One minute, I think I'll do it, and the next I can't imagine myself living there again, at least, not all the time. Don't worry, Analinda, you'll be one of the first to know when I make up my mind. Besides," she said with a grin, "if I do go back to Florida, you can come to visit, wrestle alligators and chase mosquitoes with a palm frond if you want."

With that, she clapped her wide-brimmed cotton hat on her head, gathered up her satchel and purse, and left her friend standing there with her mouth hanging open in shock.

She went about her daily rounds as usual, but the thought of returning to Florida kept her close company. That weekend, she met some friends for coffee at the Santa Anna Coffee Emporium and talked it over with them.

"It's not like I need the responsibility, you know," she said to her friend Lucy. "I have tenure here and more work than I know how to handle, plus y'all, (several in the group snickered at the southernism, which she ignored). Besides that, I can retire. There's just something about that place that keeps calling me back. Frankly, I feel like a yo-yo: one minute I'm moving back home, the next, I'm staying here... then I think I can do both. Somebody help!"

Her friends laughed at her dilemma. It was like her to talk through major decisions without ever hearing what they had to say. Finally Lucy, the most outspoken of the group, spoke, saying, "BJ, you're going home to Florida. You know it, and we know it. It's not like you can't come back to visit or even continue your research if you want. This way, you'll finally have the money to allow yourself some flexibility."

"And *then* we can come to Florida on visits and stay with you", said Margaret with a grin.

"Only if I can do the same when I come back here," she shot back, smiling. She loved this group of women, and she would miss them dearly, but now she knew what they already knew—she was going home.

"One question," said Analinda in a conspiratorial whisper as they left the café, "Is there a man involved? I keep hearing something running in the background that you are keeping under cover."

BJ winked at her and replied, "Maybe, but that's not why I'm going home. You'll know soon enough!"

* * *

BJ made plans to fly to Florida for spring break, and found she was inclined to make it permanent when she retired at the end of the spring semester. She could put the house in Santa Fe up for sale in March, and then hope it moved by the time she needed to leave. Rafe was acting as steward of the inheritance in her absence and sending regular reports, but she put one of the new restoration projects on hold until she could be there in person to provide oversight. She and Rafe presented her decision to suspend work temporarily to the board via conference call, but as she did it, she felt a chill snake down her back. Something was wrong in that boardroom and she knew it, but what was it?

"Where did that come from?" she asked herself. She had learned long ago to pay attention to those warning signs, knowing they always meant something was up.

"Before we hang up, I'd like a report on Wakulla Beach," she said, stalling. "I believe that land is held in partnership with the State, right?"

George Hanson, one of the board members and an old-time resident of the river, answered, "Yes, BJ—this is George, and may I say it's good to have you on board with us. We're working in cooperation with the State to preserve what's left of the old hotel, and the surrounding land, in an effort to prevent development down there. Looters and curious residents have pretty well messed around with it, but it's posted now. The Wildlife folks are keeping watch on it while the Coastguard goes by on a regular basis. Said they caught two folks makin' out and smokin' a bit of pot down there a week or so ago. The ranger said he almost let'em go with a warning…." He finished with a chuckle.

BJ smiled. She liked Hanson and knew he loved the wilderness just as Ben had. "Thanks, George. You sure it wasn't you and that pretty young wife you just married?"

"Aw, BJ," he said, chuckling. "Don't do that to me. Virginia would kill me if she knew I told y'all we'd been down there!"

BJ found she was grateful for the solid choices Ben had made for the board, especially Rafe Alford. There was one jarring note, though. Chesterton Jones, the former CEO of the big paper mill over in Perry wanted onboard. She worried his presence could shift the balance away from preservation and restoration to development, in spite of the strategic plan and Ben's stipulations. She called Rafe later that afternoon.

"What do you think about this, Rafe?" she said. "I remember Ben saying something about that man, and it wasn't good. He said he'd sell his soul for more land to develop with the profits. *His* big real estate company—the one that *used* to be a paper company, is the only one holding more waterfront land than us on that river. You don't suppose he's up to something, do you?"

"Well," he said, "We'll have to let the board investigate it before we take any action. I will find out whom he's been lobbying; I would expect one of them had stock in that old mill that transferred into lucrative real estate. Give me a couple of days, and I'll get back to you."

"Thanks, Rafe," she said. "I'm sorry if I've alarmed you. It's just that, well, I feel funny about it, like something's wrong. I don't know what it is, but when I get that feeling, I pay attention to it."

"That's okay by me, Girl," said Alford. "Ben always said you lived by your instincts, and if he trusted your gut, I do, too. By the way, when are you comin' down?"

"I've booked a flight for spring break," she said. "I'd like to stay down at the river house if you think it will be okay."

"My gracious, girl," he said with mock alarm in his voice. "Of course it's okay. It belongs to you, and you do not have to ask or tell me anything about it unless you want to. I'll get Lydia to send the key, which we should have done as soon as probate was finished—sorry about that. We've kept the electricity on anyway, so all you need to do is go down there, flip the switch and make yourself at home."

"Before you go, tell me, have you heard anything else about the couple caught down at Wakulla Beach?" she said.

Rafe hesitated a moment and then said, "Yes, I do know about it and since it involves the board, and I am the attorney for the young man who was caught, I will tell you: it was one of our board members' own family—his son, as a matter of fact. We got him out on bail, but he'll have to see Judge Cane. That will be public record. The woman was somebody new to me with no priors. I can't say any more than that for now."

They hung up, and with a sigh, she went back to the papers she was working on. It never failed to amaze her that some students made it through their undergraduate studies with little-to-no writing skills . . . and bent herself to making remarks with her favorite green pen. When she bit her nail, pulling it to the quick, she realized her mind had drifted to a tall man with dark skin, iron gray hair and crystal-green eyes; she was thinking about Matt Walker, wondering where he was and what he was doing.

* * *

Later in the month, she called the cat-sitter, closed her adobe house in the desert, and flew out of Albuquerque on the long flight to Tallahassee. The plane left Atlanta on time, and in roughly thirty minutes, she was gazing down at the rich green that was North Florida. She found her rivers easily from above: the St. Marks and its confluence with the Wakulla at the Gulf of Mexico; the tannin-rich Aucilla and Econfina and all their tributaries; Lake Jackson—the giant draining sinkhole, Lake Talquin, the Ochlocknee River, and of course, the queen river—the Apalachicola, home of one of the few remaining pure estuaries in America.

Again, she rented a car, this time one with all-wheel drive, and headed for the river without stopping for groceries. She could run to the IGA in Woodville in the morning, but for now, she just wanted to see as much as she could before darkness fell.

Rambling down back roads barely remembered from her youth, she took her time, enjoying the strange familiarity of it. Always, when she returned to Florida, she found herself amazed by how rapidly the topography changed from red clay hills to flat, limestone karst around Woodville. That change was noticeable in everything from vegetation to wildlife, and included the desperate efforts of homeowners who tried to make green lawns from the unproductive sandy soil with chemical fertilizers.

When she pulled off the main road and drove down the sandy track to Taylor's Run, the old house with the widow's lookout perched on the top loomed ahead in the gathering fog. Cutting the engine, she listened to the silence and relaxed into it. She had almost forgotten just how big the old house was, sitting high on its native cypress pilings. Rope thick as her wrists had held those great logs in place for generations. Underneath was Ben's much-used blue and white Jeep Wagoneer with the running boards—he'd been in his wife, Nora's, Lincoln when he crashed, and she wondered if it would start after sitting unused for months.

Chapter 4

BJ found the house was clean, just as Rafe said it would be, and when she opened the floor to ceiling windows and French doors, a warm, soft breeze blew in over the marshes from the Gulf nearby, bringing with it the musty smells of the sea. She took her time to settle in, drifting from room to room. It looked almost as though Ben still lived there—everything was in its place down to a worn and faded plaid flannel shirt draped across a straight-backed chair, his battered bush hat still on its peg, and worn boots on the mat by the door. Out of respect and a lingering sense of reverence, she kept everything as it was, relishing the old man's presence, thumbing through his books and carefully placing them back on the shelves exactly as they had been.

It was quiet on the river, almost lulling her into an early evening, but that was not to be: Matt was still in Miami, but her other neighbor, Ben's close friend Bobbie Ann Rice, was expecting her to call.

"Bobbie Ann, it's me, BJ," she said, smiling at the warmth in the older woman's happy response. "Shall I pick you up for supper? I don't want you to cook—it's on me."

"Why, goodness gracious girl, you're here, and so soon!" said Bobbie Ann. "When you made up your mind you did it quick, didn't you? I'm glad you're here."

"I'm only here for a week," she said. "This isn't the real move—it's only spring break. I took advantage of the time to come down and check things out, and to see if I think I can live in this deserted outpost of civilization!"

"BJ, you hush up talkin' like that," said Rice. "You'll get used to it in no time and wonder how on earth you ever lived anywhere but here. Come over when you're ready—I'll be here. Take your time."

BJ took a shower and went out on the screened porch to comb her hair, forcing it back from her face with clips as it dried in the steamy air. Her hair had seldom been cut, but she loved it and felt a close identity with it, thinking it reflected something of the mother she had never known. Photos showed her late mother to have had the same untamed hair that she wore long and barely restrained by clips, or braided. BJ had followed suit, even as white strands invaded the black.

Feeling fresh after the shower, she donned a clean shirt and jeans, slid her feet into sandals, and left the house with a bare minimum of makeup. Smiling to herself, she reflected how different she felt here. It was a more casual lifestyle than she knew out west; makeup seemed to melt off anyway, so why bother with it?

Bobbie Ann was waiting on her porch when she got there; the diminutive woman ran out and grabbed her before she was fully out of the car.

"Child, I can't believe it's really you," she said in her southern-country voice. Pulling back from BJ, she looked at the younger woman carefully. "You're lookin' perfectly wonderful, and I'm so glad you're finally here."

BJ laughed and hugged her back. "It's good to see you, too, Bobbie Ann! I'm so glad you were home. Get your purse and let's go—I'm starved for seafood. Have you got time for Angelo's?"

"Sweetheart, I'd take fast food in a heartbeat, but Angelo's would be a rare treat." A cloud of emotion flitted over Bobbie Ann's face. "Since Ben died, I've not gone out very much."

"Oh, I'm sorry, I wasn't thinking Angelo's might be special to you and Ben," said BJ. "I knew you were close. Tell me only what you want to, but I won't ask questions, if you'd like."

Brushing tears out of her eyes, the older woman nodded as she turned, locking the door behind her.

"It's funny," said BJ, "I don't remember folks down here locking their doors just a few years ago. Have you had trouble?"

23

Bobbie Ann chuckled, saying, "Not so much since Jake Collins finally got locked behind bars down in Sanford, but I'm still careful." Her voice sobering, she continued, "His pot-diggin' in the middens, and then the thefts, finally got him in serious trouble. That last time, Ben refused to help him. It made Jake real angry, and he made threats against my Ben." Suddenly she looked over at BJ, saying, "You know, Randall Crum hasn't been able to prove it, but there's still some suspicion about the way Ben died in that car crash. It may not have been an accident, BJ. I can't hardly credit the possibility, but I wonder if somehow, Jake's crooked arm reached out from prison to hurt Ben."

Stunned, BJ hesitated and then said, "Nobody said anything about this to me, not even Rafe. What makes the sheriff think it was…?"

"Ben's death hasn't been labeled, child—didn't you know it is listed as an unsolved case?" said the woman.

"Well, no, I didn't," BJ responded in anger. "Why didn't somebody tell me before now? I would never have left. I could have stayed to try and help find out what happened."

"Well," said Bobbie Ann, trying to placate the younger woman, "There's absolutely nothing you could have done. Let's just pray Jake stays in prison for his whole term. I do *not* want to be around when he gets out next time. There's no tellin' what he'll do with Ben gone."

They spoke little until they passed through Panacea and approached the long bridge. When she saw the restaurant standing on great pilings at the water's edge, BJ exclaimed, "There it is! Look how tall it is now!"

Bobbie Ann agreed, saying, "Well, you know Hurricane Dennis tore the old one apart, didn't you? It plumb broke up and floated away, but they were able to salvage parts of it. We're just lucky that family has staying power and decided to rebuild instead of go out of business. It looks like they built this one to last."

They found a parking space, and taking the stairs to the upper level, asked for a seat on the covered porch overlooking the bridge to Alligator Point.

The host recognized BJ immediately, saying, "It's me, Rose, BJ. Where have you been all these years?" The women talked with Rose for a while, and then ordered dinner with tall glasses of sweet iced tea.

BJ was sleepy on the way back, but awake enough to see the black bear emerge from the woods just ahead, followed closely by two cubs. Laughing, she slowed down and waited for them to cross, saying, "This is what I've missed—the constant exposure to wildlife. I'm just glad I didn't collide with them."

"Well, you certainly could have if you'd been going any faster," said Bobbie Ann dryly. "They say that if you see one, it's too late to stop. We were lucky this time."

Sobered by the thought, BJ drove slower, watching for more wildlife, but the trip back to St. Marks was uneventful. She left Bobbie Ann at her door and got back to the river house in time to see the eagles fly in for the night. She climbed up to the widow's lookout as the sun set, watching as they settled in their ancestral nest atop the deadhead cypress by the dock.

The next morning, she was up and on that dock, fishing pole in hand, hoping to catch something for breakfast, but found herself too distracted by the birds and turtles to do much fishing. A great blue heron poked around in the marsh grass nearby. She was watching when it finally brought up a frog that slid slowly down its throat and then into his belly without much of a fight.

"More luck to you, big bird," she said, and gave up, laying the pole down on the dock. She dumped the earthworms she had gathered into the water and laughed when the fish that had ignored her swam to the surface for a stress-free meal.

Ben's death and the questions Bobbie Ann raised roiled to the surface, taunting her, and after breakfast, she called Rafe Alford's office.

"He's not here, Ms. Hathaway," said Miss Lydia. "He won't be in until later this afternoon. Do you want to leave him a message? He'll call you back soon as can be."

"No, no thank you," she responded, "but I would like to make an appointment for either tomorrow or the next day. It's about Ben." After hanging up with Alford's assistant, she tried Sheriff Randall Crum. The

25

officer on duty came back to the phone almost immediately, saying, "Can you come in now, Ms. Hathaway? He's here and would be right proud to see you."

* * *

Hurriedly, BJ dressed, and with quick inspiration, went down to start the old Wagoneer. She discovered the gas tank was almost empty, and barely made it to the filling station. Once there she went into shock when she discovered how much gasoline it took to fill that over-sized tank. It was fun to drive the old car, so she drove it on into Crawfordville. The needle dropped visibly with each mile she drove, and by the time she got there, BJ thought maybe she'd save it for special drives.

After a wait that included a quick read-through of the Wakulla Area Times and the Wakulla News, Crum came out, a broad smile on his face. "BJ Hathaway, I thought you were never comin' home! When'd you get here?"

She hugged the big man she had known virtually all of her life, and let him lead her into his office. They talked over coffee, and then she asked him, "Randy, Bobbie Ann tells me there's some suspicion that Ben's death wasn't an accident. Is this true?"

The laughter left his eyes as he looked at her. "I had hoped to find out what happened and tell you then, BJ. You were already back in New Mexico when the report came in: there may have been some tampering with the steering column of the car. We checked the Wagoneer out after that—else you wouldn't be drivin' it today, I can promise you. We weren't trying to keep you in the dark, I just didn't have much to tell you, and I still don't. Whoever did it, knew their business. Frankly, just between you and me, I'm hopin' Bobbie Ann will have one of her visions or dreams because at this point, we're drawin' a blank. Meanwhile, I would advise you to be careful, okay?"

She agreed and left, determined to keep in touch with the sheriff. With only two days left of her vacation, the following day she packed a picnic lunch and took the Jon boat out, floating down the river. She spent the day on the water, missing Alford's call. Mullet jumped and osprey flew overhead as she marveled at the great, belled bottoms of the cypress trees. The forest's understory was beautiful with more shades of green

26

than she could remember, and the water was crystal-clear over shimmering white sand.

Knowing them to be long gone from the river due to the mysterious loss of the apple snail, still she listened for the limpkins. She saw instead a family of wood ducks flushed by her passage. A raccoon scurried up a nearby pine, peering around at her, his bandit face a comic contrast to the beauty surrounding him.

Exhausted and happy, she pulled up to the dock at sundown, tied the boat off, and made her way up the path, admiring the house as she approached. It could not have been called beautiful by any means; there was, however, a certain aged elegance to it. The widow's walk at the roof's peak, the deep overhang and screened-in porch—all held in place by great cypress log pillars, imparted a rustic look of enduring resilience. The old house had withstood countless floods, hurricanes and a tornado or two and still, with minimal damage, managed to stay rooted in place. BJ, comforted by that knowledge, felt a sense of coming home as she walked up the steps and entered the porch.

When she flew out the next day, she knew she would be back to stay.

Chapter 5

Jake Collins heard about Ben Taylor's death through a letter forwarded to him from Rafe Alford. At first, he was excited, tearing into the heavy cream-colored envelope in his haste. Surely, by now, the old man would have let bygones be bygones. Those hopes fell away when he read Taylor's letter.

Jake,

By the time you read this letter, you will no doubt have gotten out of prison yet again. I am aware you have entertained high hopes of inheriting the river house at my death, but such is not to be. I paid your truancy fines in high school; I paid for the education you threw away; and I paid for your attorneys when you went to prison both times. It is my hope that you have now learned to pay your own way through life. There is nothing more I can, in all good conscience, give to you, because what I have left must be preserved for posterity. It, therefore, goes to BJ Hathaway, whom I know can be trusted to execute my wishes to the letter

– Ben

Angry, he crumpled the letter, threw it on the floor and stomped out to the exercise court in the blinding sunlight, tossing a basketball until he was exhausted.

A few weeks later, his stay in prison terminated due to prison overcrowding, Collins waited for the shuttle bus to pick him up from the prison yard in Sanford, Florida. It was hot in the harsh sunlight, and he longed for the thick, shady swamps of home.

Jake had almost no money left in his prison commissary fund when he left, and nowhere in particular to go, so he headed north. When he got to Tallahassee, he made his way down to the St. Marks River to Ben Taylor's place, which was like a homing beacon to him. After all, it was really the closest thing he had to a home. He figured that over-educated, big-city girl, BJ Hathaway, was long-gone by now—at least he hoped she was. If he was lucky, maybe she was still married to Greg Hathaway, had ten kids and a passel of grandchildren, and she'd stay wherever it was she was living. Or maybe not—he had yet to settle the score from high school when she scorned him in favor of Hathaway. To his way of thinking, she had taken everything he felt to be rightfully his; revenge was on his mind, and its focus was BJ Hathaway.

Walking down the drive to Taylor's Run, he picked a few blackberries. Savoring the tart sweetness, juice running unhindered down his chin, Jake made his way past the tangled underbrush. When he reached the clearing, he stopped and stared at the old house, a bittersweet taste in his craw. Set on a slight rise above the river stood a big house on cypress pilings. His grandfather had cut and driven those logs deep into the earth, he thought with pride, and his father helped build the core around which the house grew.

Collins spent many an hour in his youth atop the house on the widow's walk, watching for pirate ships, and hoping to see white pelicans flying in thermals. Later, it was Ben Taylor himself who tried to be a positive influence on the boy's life, and Collins wondered on occasion what his life might have been like had he paid attention to the old man instead of hurting him over and over.

"This should be mine," he said to himself as he strutted down the track. Ben's father bought the land from Jake's family, and designed the building himself. Jake conveniently forgot who then contracted with Jake's grandfather to build it.

As he expected, the house was unoccupied, almost as though it was waiting for him. Thick woods surrounded the perimeter of the property, hiding it from the houses on either side, but the view to the river was open through the trees. A bald eagle, high in her nest nearby, called a warning when he approached the dock.

He looked up and grinned. "So you remember do you?" he said of a boyhood prank to steal baby eaglets from the nest. "You just wait old girl—I'll get me some eaglets out of that nest yet."

Failing to notice the tire tracks etched in the sand, he walked into the clear space under the house where he saw the rusting metal chairs and glider that had been there for years. Jake paused by Ben's battered Wagoneer parked in the space next to them, and walked on. Grinning to himself, he fingered the key set high on a nail on one of the inside pilings that BJ had missed on her visit. Some things you could just count on he thought, and cackled. He flipped the fuse box on and walked up the steps, whistling.

"It's good to be free and home again," he thought to himself. "If those Miccosukee artifacts are still in that oyster shell midden where I found them, I'll have some money in a day or two and go from there. Get me a trailer or something. Meanwhile, I think I'll stay here awhile, just for old times' sake."

He climbed the steps, and let himself in, enjoying the sense of space, turned on the lights and went into the bedroom. The closet door was open and Taylor's hiking boots waited near the door, ready for a trek in the woods. The old man's floppy bush hat hung on a nail and a worn red-plaid flannel shirt lay over a straight-backed wooden chair. The air smelled of books and pipe tobacco; Jake felt the old man's presence—it made him vaguely uneasy.

He opened the wall-to-wall French doors and as always, when the doors were open with the storm shutters folded back, light flooded the place. After switching the dropped-ceiling fans on, the air quickly cooled his sweaty skin, a luxury he missed while in prison. Still restless, he lit a cigarette, seeking to banish the old man's presence by blowing his own smoke into the moving air. He found an intricately engraved copper bowl, squashed the butt into it, then lay down on the bed and took the first comfortable sleep he'd had in several years.

*　*　*

He stayed hidden at the house long enough to grow his beard and hair long and let the curly mustache droop over a scar on his upper lip—

30

the result of a scrape in high school that would be a sure give away. When he was satisfied with his disguise, he ventured down the river in Taylor's Jon boat until he found the abandoned town of Magnolia. Unloading the tools he had taken from the shed, he went to work, unearthing some pieces he expected to be there. Chuckling, he wrapped them in an old towel, and headed back to the river house. On the way back, he saw the entrance to Blackwater Creek, let the boat drift where it would and that's when he saw it: the short rise he remembered. The jungle was dark and dense with moving bogs and decaying vegetation, and trees that provided a full overhead canopy. It would be the perfect place to put a small trailer if he could find a way to get it in there.

Later that week, he contacted an old friend who specialized in Miccosukee artifacts and hitched a ride into Tallahassee to conduct some business.

"I've missed you, Jake," said Martin Sanyo, the dealer. "I could have sold more of these—in fact I did sell everything I had from the last batch you brought in. This stuff is all the rage for some of the new homeowners down here, but this work is especially fine, no cracks or scrapes. You must be taking your time now days."

Then the antiquities buyer squinted at the intricate work on the pottery and said, "This work is different from any I've seen. Where did you get it?"

Jake danced around the question without answering it. He left several thousand dollars richer than he had been when he got there, and went shopping for clothes and food.

He went to the IGA in Woodville, bought some groceries, cigarettes and beer, and caught a ride back to the river with a good ole' boy who cared nothing for who he was or where he was going.

"Get in," said Junior Crosby, who had two children up front with him. "Don't like to see no man hitchin' in this heat. You can ride in the back with the dog if you want."

Jake nodded his thanks and climbed in, riding with Crosby's long-legged Walker hound in the open bed of the truck. The dog stood at the end of a thick chain, legs stiff, and growled at him, the fur on its back raised stiff down the spine, tail spiked. Jake stared it down and finally the dog cowered in the corner as far away from him as he could get.

31

"You're right, you mangy mutt," said Jake, who hated dogs with a passion, "you get any closer to me I'll stick my knife in your ribs. You know that don't you, dog?"

The dog whimpered and buried its head in its paws as they rode in silence until Jake hopped off a mile from the river house without waving to the driver.

Crosby waved anyway, and the dog stood up as they drove away, watching Jake until he was a spec in the distance.

Not long after that, Jake felt the need for company and went down to Posey's where the St. Marks River met the Gulf of Mexico. He had gotten comfortable with the disguise now; and after several weeks of hanging around the area, folks had gotten used to him. Florida is like that—sometimes it's better to know little to nothing about the newcomers who show up on the beaches and river-ways, hang out for a while and then disappear. He was probably just another drifter passing through, and most folks paid him little heed.

A cold beer revived him and after eating a shrimp sandwich and cheese grits, he sat back, listened to the blues band playing in the corner, and watched lethargic couples play the mating dance.

He caught the eye of a big-breasted server named Robin. She had sultry hungry eyes, and after they struck up a conversation and flirted a bit, she gave him extra helpings of shrimp and grits and enough draft beer to float away. Hovering around his table, she leaned over to allow the cleavage of her breasts to catch his eye (which it did,) until the floor manager told her to serve her other customers. He knew what she wanted, and he was more than willing to help her. Sex with either men or women suited him just fine, and that worked out well in prison, but it had been a long time since he had sex with a woman; he felt himself harden in anticipation.

After she got off work, he was there, waiting for her. Her eyes went wide when she saw him leaning against the side of the building, smoking a joint. The hair on the back of her neck was damp from the kitchen, and she needed a bath, but she took a drag on the joint he offered, nodded, and led him to her car.

Saying little, they drove back into the marshes, pulled off on a side road, and had sex in the back seat with the doors open. While the

32

conditions were not exactly ideal, the sex and a little crystal meth that Jake had scored on the side made him feel like a man again. Meth, while he could take it or leave it, always did that for him in the past and it worked now for both of them. Jake took to meeting her several times a week, always bringing a small offering of drugs in exchange for the sex.

"Hey, Robin, I got a proposal for you," said Jake one night, with a big smile on his face. She turned to him, an expectant look on her face.

He realized what he'd done and grabbed her with a kiss, "No, not marriage you silly idiot, you know I ain't the marryin' kind. I told you that. No, I've found a camper trailer, and it's in pretty good shape. Can you help me get it down into the woods? We can be real private that way."

He watched her under partially closed lids, knowing she wouldn't refuse him, but he let her play with it for a bit. The woman pouted for a while, and then reluctantly agreed to help him, just as he knew she would. She borrowed her uncle's all-wheel-drive truck, and together, hauled the little yellow camper trailer— paid for with the proceeds of his pot digging, into the deep, dense woods and set it up on the rise he'd found earlier.

"Hey," he said not long after they got a generator with her tip money, "we could make some easy money down here, you know, makin' dope. I'm bringin' some cash with the pot diggin' over in Magnolia, but that's pretty much the luck of the draw. I want to get you some pretty things and maybe we can go on a trip together some place. You in?"

By that time, Robin was disillusioned as to Jake's promises, but since she was hooked on drugs and Jake Collins, she agreed to the plan. Together, they began cooking meth in the complete and undisturbed privacy of Florida's back woods, which had been Jake's plan from the beginning. Overall, Jake found the operation satisfactory; only Robin and Martin Sanyo knew who he was at that point. Sanyo wanted antiquities and paid in cash. He had no idea, nor cared, where Jake was staying, what he did or how he got the artifacts. As with Sanyo, Robin knew almost nothing about his operation. It mattered little to her as long as she had two things, sex, and the drugs Jake provided. For that, she bought or stole the supplies they needed, prepared food, and kept her mouth shut about the pot digging and meth-cooking operation.

Chapter 6

Jake yawned, batting at a fly with the folded newspaper he was too hot to read, instead, fanning himself with the paper. He knew he ought to be digging at the new site he'd just found over in Magnolia, but it was too damned hot to even think about wasting energy that way. He'd dug enough by now that folks might notice if anybody happened to go down that way, and he didn't want to lose any of the relics he could pull out of there. No matter, he'd go tomorrow, maybe. Then there was the sawdust pile at old man Taylor's place—there was no doubt about the goods buried in that one, even though most of it was of recent vintage, maybe Civil War forward, but there was no hurry. His granddaddy always said there were important family papers in a metal box in that pile of dust. He hoped the original deed to the land at Taylor's Run was in there; that was a family myth, but it stayed in the back of his mind. One of these days, he would go diggin' back there, maybe find it and get the land back.

Too sluggish to do anything about it, he lay back on the faded sofa cushions and closed his eyes—he had forgotten how hot and humid it could be in the swamp during his years in prison. The door to the dull yellow trailer stood open, the chain clanging now and again in the sporadic breeze. A noisy generator ran full tilt nearby, pushing wasted energy to the air-conditioner trying hard to compete with the open door; neither cooled the tiny trailer hidden under the trees on Blackwater Creek.

The swamp sweltered at 95 degrees and 98% humidity. Almost nothing moved under the relentless noonday sun—even the dragonflies were still, trying to survive the wet heat. Restless, hot and irritated, he took a beer from the refrigerator and went outside, hoping fresh air would help. It didn't. Listless, he shrugged, lit a cigarette, and slumped into a lawn chair, dragging on the slender white stick like it was a lifesaver. Camping in the swamp, he thought, was a small sacrifice to pay for the profit he was bringing in, but the heat and bugs in the summer were hard on a man.

Blackwater Swamp, he knew, got its name from the tea-colored water produced by the acidic tannin from cypress trees and decaying vegetation. Dense jungle, it was a miasma of sabal palms and swamp palmetto, water tupelo and willow, thick vines, rare orchids, swamp lilies, bog buttons and in places, rare pitcher plants, but Jake saw none of this. His only reason for being there now was business, so he tolerated it for that reason alone.

Collins was fast developing a lucrative methamphetamine operation that provided quick and easy profit and was more reliable than pot digging, which was often the luck of the draw. His operation was so far off the beaten track, and difficult to navigate that most folks barely knew that part of the tangled jungle existed which made it ideal for his purposes. He neither knew, nor cared, who owned the land, and apparently, no one else did either.

He pretty much had what he needed to run his business in the tiny camper trailer. It had a small bed, a half-bath with a commode that he drained into the Blackwater creek, a kitchenette complete with a small camp stove and refrigerator, and a tiny built-in sofa and table.

Lulled by the heat, he leaned back in the lawn chair and dozed off, waking quickly at the slam of a car door nearby. It was Robin. It irritated him that she might have seen him jump; no way could he let her see him as weak. It also bothered him that the damned generator made so much noise he didn't even hear the car until she slammed the door.

He ignored her and flipped the cigarette butt into the dark water lapping at the cypress knees nearby. Without speaking to the woman, he watched it float away to join the others clustered around the cypress knots.

Accustomed to his ways, Robin set about unloading the car while he watched her under half-closed lids. She leaned over the seat of the blue two-door coup, revealing a tantalizing view of long, tanned legs and the fleshy lobes of her buttocks as the shorts rode up, but still, he said nothing. Finally, she looked around at him as she backed out of the car, grimaced, and then walked slowly to the dirty trailer with her load: a big slouch purse over one shoulder, her arms filled to overflowing with plastic shopping bags. When she came back out, she stood over him, glistening with sweat.

"Thanks for getting up to help me," she said, a frown on her face. "And by the way, nice greeting—is this all I get for the chances I take for you?"

He ran his hands up her thighs and said, "You must have been to the tanning bed today. Look at you!" Leering at her darkly tinted body and sun streaked blond hair, he said, "Ain't you over-dressed for the heat today?" Already aroused, she grinned and let him pull her down to his lap.

He untied the halter strap at her neck, and taking a full breast in each hand, nuzzled his head between them, licking the perspiration. "Don't complain, Girlie—you get good pay for what you do and you know it. Besides, it looked like you was doin' okay to me. I was just enjoyin' the view."

When he kissed her, long, deep and slow, his scraggly beard scratched, but Robin didn't care, she liked it. She curled up around him, ready for more, and he laughed—she was always like that—ready for sex any time, any place. He was tempted, but then he pulled back and pushed her away, all business for now.

Standing up, he pushed her off his lap and said, "You get the stuff?"

Irritated, she answered, "I got it this time, but I gotta be careful, Jakey—old man Stafford down at Beaufort's Pharmacy is gettin' kind of cagey. Wouldn't sell me more than two boxes of cold medicine even though I told him I was bad sick. I went to a couple more places closer to Tallahassee that don't know me so well and bought the ephedrine pills first, and then took what I couldn't buy. If I get caught it'll be a long time before you get any pussy out of me, Baby." She leaned against him again, pouting, and nestled her head in the curve of his neck, the heat of her sweaty body joining his.

Rubbing her back, Jake spoke into her ear, "You ain't gonna get caught, Baby, you're too good for that." He nibbled her ear, playing it with his tongue.

Disentangling herself, Robin shivered. Moving in a languid saunter, she went inside. Jake followed her, and stood in the door, watching. She was getting antsy and needed a hit, and would need it soon. Sultry and nervous at the same time, she pulled her damp hair up into a clip and set to work. Carelessly she stacked boxes on top of boxes until the entire contents threatened to fall out of the cabinet. Finally, she gave up and slammed the flimsy door. She flipped the empty plastic bags onto the miniscule sofa and flopped down beside them. Leaning back, she unzipped the tight denim shorts and pulled the back strings of her damp halter-top loose, dropping it on top of the plastic bags. She stretched at the freedom as her breasts lay exposed to the moist air and her belly relaxed. Pushing the wet hair up off her forehead, she mopped the sweat off her skin, and said, "How can you stand this place, day in and day out, Jake? There must be a better place to cook than this snake-infested swamp! We ought to move over to Lake City. I've got an uncle over there that might let you put this dump on his property if I ask him real nice. He's even got a cute little house I bet he'd let us live in. Besides, I think folks are catchin' onto what I'm doin' even if they don't know who I'm doin' it with, and I'm scared to death of gettin' caught and goin' to jail."

Lounging against the open door, he ignored the part about moving the trailer and instead focused on her comment about jail, saying, "Speakin' of jail, what's this about you and that Jones boy makin' out down at the Wakulla Beach ruins? The word is that his daddy bought him out of some trouble and that it was you he was playin' with down there." His eyes narrowed, "You'd better not play around on me girl, not with him or anybody else. I guarantee you'll regret it—I will kill him, and maybe you, too."

The sudden chill in his voice dripped with venom, and she looked up at him, fear in her dark eyes and in her voice, "Jake, you weren't here when that happened—surely you know that. Besides, he didn't mean anything to me, not like you do, Baby. I haven't been with anybody else since I hooked up with you."

Jake looked at her for a moment, considering what she said, then roughly pushed her over and sat down. Ignoring the plastic bags sticking to his legs, he began to lick the salty sweat off her skin again, rubbing her inner thighs just a bit too hard. "I know you won't slip around on me," he said, still in that soft, deadly voice, "and you better not get caught takin' the stuff I need either, Baby Girl."

She watched him, mesmerized by the venom in his voice and the steel in his hands.

"Now, let me give you a little reward for working so hard for Daddy," he said, changing his tone. Sulking, she hid her face in his neck as he pulled out his pipe, then watched with interest as he packed it with meth and lit it, her eyes mere slits as she watched it melt. Childlike, she took it eagerly, sucking it like a lollipop. Then, licking her lips in anticipation, she inhaled deeply, heavily lined eyes now closed and relaxed.

Jake waited a few minutes, watching, then pulled at one ripe breast, worrying at the nipple, pinching it to see what would happen. She groaned at his touch, and then twisted toward him, but he wanted to make her wait until the drug took its full effect.

He pushed her back saying, "You just sit here and smoke, Baby. You'll feel better in a minute and then we'll do some stuff, okay?" Reluctantly, she nodded then closed her eyes, inhaling the sweet poison that felt so good; it expanded her senses and banished any inhibitions she had left.

He pulled away and left her while she made the hit. That batch, laced with ecstasy was an experiment and he wanted to see how long it would take to work. He turned and watched her from the doorway again for a few minutes, feeling his own need grow as the drug took effect on her. It always did that to him, watching her turn on like that.

Her dark eyes were open now, looking at him, pupils dilated, her legs spread wide, waiting for him. He went back to her and when he touched her, she responded immediately, moaning and ready: no foreplay required. Pulling her up, he half led, half dragged her to the bed, pulling her shorts down her thighs as they went. She tore at him, wild with need.

"Let me show you how Daddy likes his little girl," he said. Roughly, he pushed her down onto the dirty sheets, dropped his shorts and fell on her. Gripping her butt hard, he grabbed a breast with his teeth and bit her. She screamed as he entered her without preliminary. What he had to give was quick in coming, but when he rose, sweating and spent, she lay there writhing, still orgasmic, blood dribbling from the bruised breast he had bitten.

"Don't leave me now, Jake," she pleaded. "I need more. Please don't go. It's never been like this before. I'm goin' crazy with it, please…"

He laughed and told her, "Do it yourself, *Sweetheart,* you know how," and swaggering in his maleness, he left her jerking, still screaming in sexual agony in the stale air of the hot bedroom. He took a cold beer from the refrigerator and walked out of the trailer naked, feeling a slight breeze on his sweaty skin, whistling. It felt good to be out like this, free and wild like an animal, he thought to himself.

Robin lay, still orgasmic, in the sordid heat of the damp, soiled bed linens. In the twilight of agony, she wanted more sex, wanted out, wanted God knows what. It seemed the hit lasted for hours. Oblivious to the heat and the flies that clustered over her sex, she was finally conscious only of incessant throbbing between her thighs and wasted tears oozing onto the dingy pillow.

* * *

Jake finished his beer and threw the can at a turtle that quietly slid off its log and disappeared in the dark water. The can joined the others floating with the cigarette butts at the base of the cypress knees. He stayed outside for a while smoking a joint, and then went inside to see what was happening with Robin. He had listened to her extended agony with pleasure, and thought the meth and ecstasy mix satisfactory. With the chemicals he needed to cook with getting harder to find, it would be necessary to diversify and concoct other mixes to satisfy his market, and he wanted to find an easier way to make it. He smiled thinking of how to push his newest creation, knowing he could sell it, and where—there was a new bar opening down in Panacea, and next week was the grand opening. He would be there, in disguise, of course.

He stood in the doorway until she became aware of him. She rolled over and opened her legs to him, the mixture of semen and sticky sweat glistening in her pubic hairs, blood crusted on the bruised breast. She was coming down from the high, but still he entered her, again without foreplay. She flew at him with passion renewed. He emptied himself into her like water down a drain. He knew it hurt when she cried, but he was only giving her what she wanted, and she dammed well ought to appreciate it.

When she finally lay quiet under him, he stayed on top of her for a few minutes, contemplating what else he could do, but it was hot and stuffy in the small room. He moved away, pulled his shorts on, yanked a T-shirt from its hook near the bed, grabbed his boots and took off through the cypress knees and down to old man Taylor's Jon boat. He left without speaking to the woman in the trailer, stopping only to close the door to keep out the hordes of mosquitoes descending with twilight.

Chapter 7

Her decision about retirement and plans for the move to Florida made public, BJ's friends planned a combined retirement/going-away party in her honor. While flattered by the party plans, BJ found she was anxious to be on the road as soon as she finished packing the truck. Deciding to keep the adobe house for the time being, she leased it to a graduate student, leaving minimal furnishings for him. The rest she divided between storage and the rental truck.

Eagerly, she made layouts of the river house and its rooms, planning where to place her own things, knowing she wanted to keep the essence of Ben Taylor intact. Her books, research materials and artwork would make the move. Some things she divided between her friends—easily the most difficult to part with in the move south.

Finally, all was ready and departure imminent. Analinda and her other friends were there to see her off and she drove away, glancing in the rearview mirror from time to time to see them and her beloved home as long as she could.

* * *

Paddling, Jake made his way slowly out of the swamp, skirting twisted tree roots and downed trees, ducking under wild grape vines as thick as his legs. He drifted down Blackwater Creek, first using the paddle, and then onto the St. Marks River where he pulled the motor to life and made his way to the river house.

He cut the motor and drifted into the cove, pushed the small boat deep into the reeds near Taylor's dock. Neatly avoiding a water moccasin that had taken to sleeping on the bottom step, he walked up the limestone rock path to the river house with sure feet. He'd been going there regularly since he got back, using it as adjunct housing to the trailer in the swamp. He figured the old man owed it to him.

Laughing, he kicked a can out of his way and climbed the steps, cursing the security light as it came on. "I'll have to remember to disconnect that son of a bitch one of these days," he thought to himself, "but not tonight."

He knew all about the place—virtually everything. He had made it his business to know these things when old Ben took pity on him a couple of years back, letting him work around the place to help pay off some debts; that was after he got out of Raiford the first time. Since his return, he had explored everything on the property with an eye for things he could use or sell.

Chuckling, he thought about Ben Taylor and knew he would be furious if he knew that of all people, Jake Collins was abusing his hospitality, and he would be especially angry if he could see what it looked like now. It had taken very little time for Jake to trash the old house, and he went at it with determined intent. Bait buckets and beer cans littered the steps, cigarette butts dotted the ground like confetti, and the screened door was hanging half-off its hinges. Inside, roaches, big fat ones, satiated from open tins of tuna and Spam, bags of chips and half-empty beer cans ignored him. The place smelled of rotting food, stale tobacco, sweat and urine. He used his bare arm to push some of the mess into the overflowing trash bin at the end of the counter, laughing when it overflowed to the floor and the roaches scattered. He went into the bedroom, stripped, took a shower and then crawled naked into the old man's bed, feeling a sense of satisfaction and power.

Two hours later, he got up for a much-needed beer, lit another cigarette and looked around for something to sell, speculating on what Ben's prized projectile-point collection would bring up in Atlanta, New York or even Europe and Asia. He knew some of those museums cared only for the treasure, not how they got possession. His disposal and distribution network was in place: he knew who was the most aggressive in their need to possess rare antiquities, and who had fattest pockets. He wasn't especially worried about discovery, as they would pay and do almost anything to get their hands on what he had to offer. He was wily as a snake and proud of it.

42

Jake stood at the door to Ben's bedroom studying the mounted projectile point display that hung directly behind the bed. Disposing of it would take a special trip in daylight and would require some planning to avoid detection. Maybe Martin Sanyo would broker this one for him.

He had sold a couple of things from the house to a newcomer down on Alligator Point just the week before. They were decorating their place and could probably use some more pieces, but something made him cautious about selling too much to one buyer, especially something this valuable. He had no idea to what era the points belonged; he did know, however, that it was a highly prized and would fetch a high dollar amount.

Chapter 8

Bobbie Ann Rice pushed her sleeves up and leaned back in the small pontoon boat. Lulled by the gentle movement of the water, late afternoon heat and the sound of dragonfly wings buzzing overhead, she felt drowsy, soothed by the hypnotic effect of the river. She was almost asleep when an osprey flew directly overhead, landing in its nest on top of a rusty, defunct railroad bridge that spanned the St. Marks River.

Working on an assignment for a nature magazine, she left home just after dawn to be with the sun when it rose. She spent the day on the water, exploring the side creeks and bends of the old stream with far-seeing eyes, taking photographs of the old trees she found on its banks. As she neared the confluence of the St. Marks and Wakulla Rivers, she watched for the manatees that swam in the Wakulla River's spring fed waters. Letting her hand drift just above the water's surface, she smiled when a mother and pup approached the boat. She sat up just enough to rub the pup's soft, leathery skin before it sank again, following its mother to deeper water.

The water was so clear and clean she could see individual grains of sand sparkling like shimmering crystals in the falling sun. Suddenly, a sharp stab of grief hit her and tears flowed unchecked. The last time she took this trip, Ben was with her; now she had only memories of that journey. She held them close and cherished each one, but at times, the pain of his death was overwhelming.

I've got to work past this, she thought. Ben is still with me; I expect to hear his voice or feel his touch at every bend in the river. How can I deal with his death without forfeiting the memories we shared?

The air was still warm at sunset. Clouds of mosquitoes left stinging welts as she drifted along, but for the most part, she ignored them. They were maddening, but they were part of the place with no real escape on the river's channel. She pulled her hat down low, pushed her sleeves down over her hands, and kept moving; it was time to go home—alone.

She was half-way there when she remembered she was supposed to have dinner with friends at Posey's in Crawfordville, but there was nothing she could do about it. Cell phones failed to work in that swampy wilderness. Hungry, she prayed they understood when she got there for dessert.

Late afternoon's golden light shifted on the marsh grasses, turning them from soft dusty green to golden and then coppery brown and coral in stark contrast to the dark blue waters of the waterway.

She caught her breath as a sturdy silver fish, a mullet, sprang into the air just ahead, landing with a belly flop and a loud splash. She laughed as it hit the water—the act of jumping looked free and effortless, and she wondered if the fish rejoiced in the leap. The canopy of water tupelo, black gum, and water willow formed a tunnel overhead as the old stream turned and disappeared from sight in the darkening light. In stark contrast, white crinum lilies, their soft spidery white blossoms held by deep green foliage, glowed from the dark forest floor, and giant ferns and palm fronds fell from the river's banks. Tree roots, intertwined like ancient fingers held the water in the streambed. She fumbled for the digital recorder, longing for enough light to write instead.

Darkness dropped like a cloak under the dense canopy of trees. She shivered as the sun completed its fall below the horizon. Thick fog condensed in the cooling air and with it came a vague sense of unrest. An owl hooted nearby, its wings flitting through the trees. The call of the watcher spooked her, just as when she first heard it in the wilderness. Shivers snaked down her spine as the big bird hooted again, staying with her as she quietly motored down the river. Chilled, she took off her life jacket, adding a heavy flannel shirt to make another layer. Still uncomfortable in the dense fog, she added a waterproof, quilted jacket over all and finally felt warmth creep back into her tired bones.

As she approached the mouth of Blackwater Creek, she noticed the foul smell again, a sickly, sweet odor that had nothing to do with the

45

detritus of a natural ecosystem. Early that morning when she passed the entrance to the creek, she saw yellowing on some of the trees and a strange dieback in places. Something was wrong on Blackwater Creek, and she would need to document what she had seen for the Florida Wildlife folks in the coming week.

Peering into the darkness, a dim light shimmered in the distance, but with the fog, she couldn't be sure *what* she was seeing. There were no homes in this part of the boggy swamp—she knew that. She was also aware that nobody in their right mind would dare camp in there, as the peat bogs were unstable throughout much of the region. Was the illusive and famed Wakulla Volcano making an appearance again? Now, she wondered if there really had been something percolating in the swamp, then shook her head. No, it was probably just steam from the bog.

A small herd of deer, barely visible at the water's edge, faded into the darkness, and the glint of red eyes on the water's surface reminded her that alligators peopled the river.

Dense fog hid the rising moon, shrouding the woman and her boat, a mysterious barge on ghostly waters, making it difficult to see in the distance, but she pushed on, sure of her destination. At last, Ben Taylor's dock appeared suddenly out of the dark. It occurred to her then that she couldn't recall seeing Ben's boat earlier in the day, but there it was, securely tied up at his dock. Again, she saw soft light wavering in the distance, this time in the direction of Ben's place, and then it was gone.

Puzzled, she thought, what is going on? First, there was that funky smell, then dieback in the swamp, the 'light,' at Blackwater Creek, Ben's boat, and now another light in the distance.

Perhaps it was just the illusion of moonlight shimmering through the fog, she thought. Still uneasy, she stared into the darkness, wishing for the flashlight she left behind earlier in the day. At last, she bumped her way around the cypress knees and found her own dock. Peering through the heavy mist towards Ben's place, she tried to find the light again, but all was dark. She shook her head, got the bag with her camera, the recorder, and her notebook, and climbed out. She felt her years as she tied the boat, gripped the stick she always used and felt her way up the walkway, staggering on legs left still far too long. Bobbie Ann Rice found herself weary to the bone, ready for a hot bath and ravenous.

46

When Matt Walker finally made his way back home to North Florida, he timed his arrival to coincide with BJ's. Collecting Chi (an orphaned chow-shepherd) from the vet in Crawfordville, he went home to await the call from BJ, who should be arriving sometime after sunset.

For once, BJ was too tired to care that she could not see Thomasville, Georgia's magnificent plantation lands with their stands of ancient live oak and long-leaf pine. Determined, she pushed through South Georgia and over the line into Florida.

When she finally called to let Matt know she was on the approach, her voice was eager, almost like that of a schoolgirl coming home from college, "Matt, I just crossed the famous state line into Florida. Are you home yet?"

"Yeah, I got in this afternoon, picked Chi up from the vet and went to the grocery store," he said in that warm, crusty voice she knew so well. "Do you want me to meet you when you get close to the crossroads at St. Marks?"

Exhausted from three days of driving a moving van, she was grateful for the help and eager to see him. It was past midnight when she arrived, but Matt was waiting for her when she turned at the light onto HWY 98. She flashed her lights, waved, and made her way home to the river house. He followed her, Chi sitting in the passenger seat, looking for all the world, like another person riding shotgun.

Chapter 9

Sleepy, Jake turned on the ceiling fans, opened the French doors, and lay down again. High in the tree line, eye level with the old sabal palms and moss-covered live oaks, it was cooler and he could rest. That was the last he knew until later that night, when he was roused by a sound outside. He awoke on full alert. It was just past midnight.

Somebody was coming, and he didn't much feel like getting caught. He pulled on his shorts and T-shirt, grabbed his boots and crept out through the French doors, released the torn screened door and made his way down the back steps like a cat.

Car lights shown on the steps as he stealthily moved towards the bottom step. He heard several car doors slam, then watched as two people approached the dark house. He stifled an insane giggle as they stumbled on the litter accumulated in the yard. Angling behind one of the double-log cypress pilings, he stayed just outside of the beam of light and cursed when he saw it was BJ Hathaway and an unidentified male.

The security light flipped on as they began to climb up the front stairway, clearing debris as they went. Pausing briefly, with an imperceptible motion only the occupant of the car could see, Walker signaled Chi; the dog jumped quietly from the open door and came, eyes on his master, anxious to track. Walker signed, "Quiet, search" and the big red dog left them without a sound.

Jake waited, thinking himself hidden. He watched as the couple slowly made their way up the stairs in grim silence. He could see the man was tall and muscular—not someone he wished to tangle with at night. Hathaway, however, was another question; he had matters to settle with her and relished the thought of her comeuppance.

Just as Walker opened the porch door, Chi sank his teeth into the exposed flesh in the back of Jake's bare thigh. He neither saw nor heard the dog—the attack took him completely by surprise. Yelling, he lit out for the river with the big red dog snapping at his heels. Out of breath and desperate to escape, he jerked the boat out of the reeds, pushed it into the river and jumped in after it, arms flailing. Grabbing the oars, rowing as fast as his arms would move, he pushed hard, afraid of pursuit though none came. Chi panted at the water's edge, with what looked like a happy smile on his funny, black-muzzled face, the long, black and purple tongue dripping with saliva.

Jake made it into the current and let the boat drift as he fumbled, trying to pull the motor to life. Cursing, he jerked the paddles and rowed without stopping. Heedless of the pain in his thigh and the blood pooling at his feet, he pushed on until he noticed bumps appearing in the water around him. Red, glowing, hungry eyes stared as he went by—gators! That's all he needed— damned gators following him home intent on an early breakfast. Afraid to slow down, he worked the oars with all his strength until he finally pulled into Blackwater Creek and slowed to a stop. Startled by his arrival, a flock of snowy white egrets, asleep in a tree nearby flushed and cawed, then flew deeper into the tree's infrastructure and settled their feathers again. Slowly, they faded into the background, ghostly specters watching from a distance. Now more curious than afraid, the big birds stared down at him as he climbed out of the boat. Hollering and banging on the sides of the boat and the cypress knees with the oar to frighten potential attackers, Jake stumbled as a horned owl hooted and flew directly overhead, the great wings nearly brushing his hair.

"God dammed owl. If I had my gun you'd be dead," he screamed, running and stumbling to get away from the danger in the water and overhead.

Not until he was well into the trees did he begin to relax. Tonight, there was a sense of menace and something palpable in the air on Blackwater Creek. Frightened, his heart pounding, he groped about in the darkness, no longer sure of himself, trying to find his way to the tiny trailer and Robin. The ancient magnolia that gave shelter to the yellow camper also prevented the moon's gentle light from exposing it. The lights were out and the trailer was dark and barely visible as he approached it. The generator was quiet. Robin must have turned it off in the cool of the night or it ran out of fuel.

Since he was coming in from the river, her car, parked under the camouflage canopy on the other side of the trailer, was invisible. He didn't care if she was there or not. He just wanted to get inside and away from the gators and night sounds that had followed him all the way from Ben Taylor's river house. Again, he heard the rustle of wings nearby and thought to himself, "That idiot owl—I'd kill it with my bare hands if I could see it," and stumbled up the steps and into the trailer.

* * *

Matt and BJ stood at the top step to the house, quiet in the moonlight, watching as the thin man with the pale hair ran down to the water, jumped into the boat and paddled away. He looked familiar but not enough to distract Matt from the job at hand. He called Chi and waited until the dog bounded up the stairs and rejoined them. They roughhoused a bit, congratulating one another on a job well done, then the man and woman walked through the warped screened door and onto the porch.

The door to the kitchen was open. Unprepared for what she saw, BJ caught her breath when Walker flipped the light switch. Beer bottles and cans, cigarette butts, half-burned joints and trash covered every surface. The fetid odor of urine lingered in the air.

Hordes of big cockroaches ran for cover when the light hit them, spilling out of the cans and open bags of chips. "Who was that man? What on earth is going on here?" BJ said to Matt, then cried, "This is desecration!"

The air was stale from tobacco smoke and spoiled food and BJ felt the urge to vomit too strong to ignore. Nauseous, she stalked into the bathroom, took one look at the moldy commode, backed onto the porch, and retched over the railing. It appeared the river house—Taylor's Run, had been occupied and ridden hard since she was last there. Further exploration revealed filthy sheets and soiled towels, but she was bone tired from driving the moving van for several days—much too tired to do anything about it now.

"Come home with me, BJ," said Walker. "It's too late to find a motel," and peering into the darkness on the other side of the house, added, "I would expect Bobbie Ann has been asleep for hours. Surely you don't want to stay here until Randy has had a chance to check it out."

Exhausted, angry and dismayed by what they had found, BJ agreed. "This is not exactly the kind of homecoming I was expecting," she said with a bitter taste in her mouth, "but I can see that coming back here was the right decision. I'm glad I'm here." She turned to Matt and added with steel in her voice, "You know I won't stop until I find out who did this, don't you?"

"I would expect nothing less," he said, grinning. "If you'll let me, I will help. We all will, you know that." They agreed to wait to call Sheriff Randall Crum until morning. "Whoever that was, he's not likely to return tonight," said Matt with a grin. Absently, she nodded and walked to the truck to get her overnight bag and Martha's carrier. Securing the rental for the night, she joined Matt and Chi for the trip out to HWY 98, and then back down the long drive to his place.

* * *

Conscious of the matted blood draining from his leg as he walked, Jake stumbled in the dark, trying to find his way in the dark trailer. Robin hated the swamp at night and usually kept the generator going, playing the boom box when he left her alone, but this time there was silence. He cursed as the owl hooted just outside, close enough to spike gooseflesh.

"Hey, Robbie, wake up, I'm in trouble here, you gotta help me," he called. Getting no answer, he groped around in the dark for the flashlight. The woman lay in the bed where he left her hours before, curled up in a fetal position. He nudged her, saying, "Hey, Girl, it's me, wake up." Slowly, she began to move, uncurling herself. A strong stench came up to greet him as she unfolded. He grimaced at the sight and smell saying, "God, you could have taken a shower or something; this place stinks like a whore house! Get up and help me. I'm hurt real bad."

She opened her eyes slowly and at first, even in his angst, he saw the unfocused flicker of something very much like hatred in her eyes

51

before the shutters flipped down. She turned away from him, groaning, and said, "What the hell did you put in that meth, Jake Collins? I thought I was dyin' out here in this stinkin' swamp right by myself. How could you do that to me after what I've done for you? You can't even drive out of this God forsaken place without a disguise—I'm your eyes, ears and hands and you give me laced meth. Some thanks I get."

He leaned into her and said, "Well, you gotta admit the sex was hot stuff, wasn't it? Sometimes you gotta lose things to get somethin' that good."

She shrugged him away, saying, "Yeah, it was great until you left me like that, in a full throttle that went on for almost the whole damned night. Don't you ever do that to me and leave me alone again or I'm out of here, you hear me?'

"Oh, come on, Robbie," he pleaded, "I'm hurt, I need your help. I can't even reach back there to see how bad it is."

He dropped his shorts and turned around. The woman gasped when she saw the damage Chi had inflicted and said in a thick voice, "What got a hold of you, a bear?"

"No," he said, "I was over at Ben Taylor's place," seeing the expression on her puffy face he said quickly, "I was just hangin' around—I get tired of bein' here all the time. Sometimes I just gotta get out. Anyway, BJ Hathaway and some muscle-bound pretty boy showed up, and I lit out. I got out of the house but the dammed mutt got me before I could run. How bad is it?"

Chapter 10

After leaving Taylor's Run, Matt and BJ spoke very little, each preoccupied with their own thoughts, but Matt was uneasy. His place was just as vulnerable as Ben's, but it was undisturbed when he arrived earlier that day and Chi, a retired police K9, showed no signs of alarm. His place looked just as it had when he left it months before.

Matt showed BJ to the bathroom and gave her fresh towels, and then left her alone. He opened the deep windows, flipped the ceiling fans on, and changed the sheets on the bed before lying down on the sofa. He was asleep, Chi at his feet, forgetting everything but the sweet sounds of the breeze in the trees outside the open windows. He never knew how long the tall woman watched him and the red dog before turning out the lights and going to bed.

The next morning he woke to the cackling sounds of a heron, and gulls laughing high above. Tired and disoriented from his own travel, not to mention the craziness of the night before, he first called Sheriff Randall Crum, telling him what they had found. Then he remembered his houseguest. He was about to make coffee when he heard footsteps on the stairs. Chi flew off the sofa barking, and then stopped at the door, ears cocked.

Quickly, Matt stepped into the jeans and shirt he had thrown on a chair the night before, went to the door and jerked it open, a scowl on his face. His temper changed quickly when he realized his visitor was none other than Bobbie Ann Rice, his neighbor and very good friend. She stood there, scrubbed and fresh, her plain face completely void of makeup, neat gray hair held back by a headband. In her hands, she held a tray with cups of steaming, fragrant coffee, and a bag of fresh donuts from Luella's in Crawfordville perched on the top.

"Matt, open the door right this minute," she said, demanding to be let in. "Randall Crum has got half the deputies in Wakulla and southern Leon Counties at Ben's place, and he wouldn't tell me a darn thing beyond saying there was an intruder last night. *Let me in this door right this minute, Matt Walker*—the coffee's gonna' to get cold! We need to talk right now."

When he hesitated, she stepped back, a question in her eye. Speaking rapidly she said, "Well, is this any way to greet a lady? Come on, let me in the house Matt; the mosquitoes are loggin' poison darts at me." Then she added, "Is BJ here?"

Smiling, he relaxed and opened the door, drawing her into the screened porch. Gingerly taking the coffee, he said, "Yes, she's here. Hey, I'm mad alright, but not at you. I was hoping it was Randall coming to tell us who broke into Ben's place."

Taking a swallow of the coffee, he added, "I really appreciate this, trust me—there's not much to eat in the house. Come to think of it, some of it's still out in the car, and I'll bet you the milk is spoiled."

Without saying a word, the petite woman looked at the rumpled sheets on the sofa, then at the closed-door to his bedroom, and cocked an eyebrow at him.

Smiling with mischief in her eyes, Bobbie Ann poured coffee from the foam cup into a mug, looked up at him with a crooked smile and said, "You really do look dangerous today, Matt. All you need is a scarf on your head and a gold earring. One look at you and any woman worth her salt would have to decide whether to sacrifice her virtue or give it gladly."

She was joking, but not completely: he did indeed look dangerous—sensual, and very appealing—in the rumpled half-buttoned plaid shirt and jeans, hazel eyes glittering in his deeply tanned face, the ever-present lock of stubborn gray hair curling down over one arched eyebrow.

Bending to inhale the rich scent of the coffee, she missed the look of speculation he shot her, and said, "Now, you just simmer down and drink up fast—that coffee will do you a world of good. In my opinion, you look like you are in need of it. Randall is spewing like that mysterious swamp volcano, and expecting you and BJ first thing."

Again, she glanced at the closed door and executed a 360 turn in the conversation, "Seriously, Matt, I saw the rental truck and stopped by Ben's place, thinking BJ would be there—it's the first time I've been near the place since Ben... I just haven't had the heart to go over there since he died. I was shocked, the yard's a disaster. Randall refused to allow me inside; then I figured you brought BJ over here. Knowing you'd both need nourishment, I came riding in to your rescue."

"And again, I thank you," he said, bowing before the older woman. "We planned to meet at the Coastal for a late supper, but BJ called from the road to tell me she wouldn't make it in time. I made her promise to call me when she got into St. Marks, which she did, and I met her at the crossroads and drove down to the river house with her. You know how pitch black dark it is down here this time of year."

Hearing no response from Bobbie Ann, he glanced up quickly, adding, "Don't look at me that way! I just thought she might need some help. It's a good thing she let me come, don't you think?"

Amused by his stammering response to the situation, she waited on Matt, who for once seemed to be discombobulated; it was taking him forever to tell her what she wanted to know. Her eyes widened as he described the encounter from the night before, but still, she said nothing.

"Whoever did that needs to suffer, and frankly, I couldn't care less if the gators got him when he lit out," he said. At her expression he added, "Don't worry, we left the place as it was and called Randy. He told us to come over here in case the perpetrator tried to return. I haven't seen or heard from Randy or BJ this morning. She must have slept like the dead last night. Surely Randy knows we're anxious to know who it was, and I'm wondering if it's somebody we know."

He peered through the line of trees between the properties and said, "I'm going to clear some of that undergrowth between these two houses, and I'll help do the same on the other side if you'll let me. I don't like to think that man has been messin' around at Ben's place with no interruption, and you couldn't even see the lights from your house. What if he had come to your place?"

55

The thought was disconcerting to Bobbie Ann, too. She hadn't given any thought to her own potential for danger.

They heard the shower running and quietly discussed the mess at the River House, while they waited for BJ to join them.

"As soon as Randy gives us the go ahead, I'm going to help her clean that crap out of there," he continued, staring out at the river, "but first, we've got to see if he knows who it might be."

He looked away from the river, and saw the look on Bobbie Ann's face. He stopped short, saying, "What's the matter? What's wrong?"

She felt numb and looked at him with eyes filled with fear. "Matt, I took the Jon boat down to the lighthouse yesterday—I was out all day, and it was dark when I got in last night. I saw a light up there, but then it disappeared. I thought I was just seeing things. You don't think I saw… "

His voice was harsh when he said, "Good God, you were out there by yourself? You might have been killed!"

Surprised by the vehemence in his voice, she responded with, "I am, after all, a nature writer, Mr. Walker, and being alone in the wilderness is part of my job," she said, her voice dripping with sarcasm.

When he failed to answer, she returned to the issue at hand, "I haven't noticed a thing from my place, at least not 'til I saw that light last night. Surely, there will have been other episodes in the area, wouldn't you think? Ben's isn't the only place that has been trashed, is it?"

He answered, "Well, I haven't been home in several months and my place looks just like it did when I left it. You live on the other side of Ben's and until last night you didn't see or hear anything either. No, I think this was deliberate and from the looks of it, I believe it's because it *is* Ben Taylor's place.

Bobbie Ann went down to her truck and brought the camera back up for Walker to see the photos she had taken the day before. Together, they pored over them and this time, seeing them after a night's rest, Bobbie Ann felt even more rattled by what she saw—murky water at the mouth of the creek, dying trees and yellowed vegetation. Where was the pollutant coming from?

56

Matt whistled when he saw them, running his hand through unruly hair, saying, "Something is going on down here all right, and wouldn't you know it's just as BJ gets here?

Chapter 11

Even though BJ showered when she and Matt got to his place, the next morning it felt as though the foul odors from the river house clung to her still. She took yet another bath, scrubbing as if in ritual cleansing until her skin glowed from it. At last, feeling cleansed and refreshed, she stepped out to dress and was startled to hear Matt's voice in greeting. Hearing Bobbie Ann's elegant southern country accent, she grabbed one of Matt's shirts and pulled it over her pajama pants, combed her hair, twisted it up into a clip, and walked barefooted onto the porch.

"Coffee, somebody please get me coffee," she mumbled sleepily. Laughing, Bobbie Ann handed her a steaming cup of black coffee and sat her down between them.

"Oh, BJ," said Bobbie Ann, "I am so glad to see you. Matt's been tellin' me about what you found at the house last night. It never occurred to me somebody would go in and trash Ben's place like that. It plumb breaks my heart just to think about it," she added, with tears in her eyes.

They made plans to meet at the river house to clean later in the day, unless the sheriff gave them early clearance. BJ went to Matt's room to dress, but not before Bobbie Ann whispered, "You be real careful with Matt, BJ. I saw how he looked at you sittin' there in his shirt."

BJ scoffed playfully, but as she turned away she asked, "Be careful of what, Bobbie Ann? What we had was good, but it is in the past, and now we are *friends*. I'm fairly certain that I am nothing more to Matt than that—an old friend. Besides, he's probably got nubile young grad students hanging off of him all the time."

"Suit yourself, BJ," said Bobbie Ann with an arched eyebrow, "but I know what I saw just now. He like to have never got over it when you broke up with him and left the last time, and I don't want to see him hurt again. Do you understand me?"

Feeling confused by everything that had happened since she arrived, and finding a need to sort things out, BJ brooded over Bobbie Ann's words into the morning. The result was that she began to create distance between herself and Matt. At first, he was too intent on the issue at hand to notice.

By mid-morning, all three were standing in the screened-in porch of the river house talking with Sheriff Randall Crum, surveying the damage as a deputy dusted for fingerprints.

"This was no random break-in folks," said the sheriff. "Somebody has been hanging out here for several weeks, and it looks deliberately trashed, to my way of thinkin'. Most transients live lightly off a place and move on in the night; they seldom break in and set up housekeeping. This looks like deep work from somebody who means real harm, and one who knows Ben won't be back." He turned to Matt and BJ and said, "Tell me what happened here last night."

BJ was staring at the house, a distracted look on her face, so Matt spoke first. "Well, in case you forgot, I've been gone for three months and just got back late yesterday. I met BJ to help her get in last night and this is what we found. My place was clean, and Chi was perfectly normal when I got him home from the vet, so I don't think anybody has snooped around there, and Bobbie Ann's place is untouched as well. With no forced entry, it looks to me like the intruder knew where everything was already, and didn't have to break in."

"Randy, when I was here a couple of months ago, this place looked just like it did when Ben was here," BJ added, a wistful sound in her voice, "and when I left, I made sure I left it that way, too. Last night, when we got to the foot of the steps and the security light came on, it was a shock. We could see the mess the yard was in, and the stuff on the steps, and I couldn't believe my eyes. It's also why we couldn't see who was out there between us and the river."

Walker agreed, saying, "Even the fridge was cold and stocked with beer, Randy. It isn't Ben's brand—somebody's been in here on a

59

regular basis for some time now, and it might be somebody who also knew I was going to be out of town. What do you think?"

"I think we'll know more when Rusty gets those fingerprints to the lab," said the sheriff. "Y'all keep thinkin' about anything that might be missing, okay? I'll call later today. Keep the phone handy," said the sheriff.

"You ready, Rusty?" he continued. "Let's head into town and find out who's been messin' around down here." He turned to BJ and said, "It'll be alright for you all to do some housecleaning now. I know that's what you want to do, right?"

The sheriff turned away, and then stopped to add, "I'm surely glad you are home, BJ." He studied the woman with the dark eyes and high cheekbones as she stared at the house that was to be her home. "Don't let this scare you off. We'll get this perpetrator and you can get on with your life. I'm gonna' set a watch down here for a while, and I want you to get a dog—a big one, and get that security system reconnected—make those your top priorities. I figure whoever that was will be back, and I don't want you here unprotected." When she protested he added, "Now, you know better than to try and tell *me* what to do, BJ Hathaway. I've been at this longer than you've been alive."

She nodded and with a grave smile extended her hand, then found herself wrapped in a bear hug from the sheriff.

She smiled again as the big man turned away, shook hands with Bobbie Ann and Matt, and left with the deputy carrying the evidence. With them gone, the three friends set about planning their cleaning strategy, knowing what the house really needed was ritual cleansing.

* * *

With BJ's blessing, Bobbie Ann brought sage and cedar, and set it to burning throughout the house, and then she called a Native American healer over in Wacissa who promised to come down later in the day to perform the cleansing of any contrary spirits who might still linger.

BJ attacked the work with vengeance, purging the evil that defiled the sacred space of Ben's home. Chi kept watch in the sun on the porch, while Martha meowed constantly from her carrier.

60

Disgust roiled in Walker's throat as he cleaned the filth from the sink, toilet, and floors. The women worked in the kitchen and the huge front room that faced the river, wondering where live roaches go in daylight.

"Last night it looked like the drag races there were so many of them," said BJ. "Now look," as she pointed to the belly-up carcasses and feces on the counters, in the sink and on the floor. Thank goodness, there are no live racers today."

Together, they removed all of the food sources and cleaned out the cabinets, disposing of everything that was potentially edible, even cardboard boxes. Then they emptied the refrigerator of all the alien beer, which Matt took down to his car. He would donate it to somebody, but the former owner of the suds was out of luck. At some point, BJ called Rafe Alford about the defunct alarm system.

Alford sounded stunned when she told him about the intrusion and asked about the alarm system. He answered her with a sheepish sound in his voice, "Why BJ, nothing ever happens down there and after six months, we let the company go. Besides, we knew by then you were coming home. . ." his voice trailed off before he said, "Look, I dropped the ball, and I am so sorry. I will come down there and clean it myself if that will help."

In a voice cooler than he had ever heard her use, BJ asked him why he made that decision without consulting her. In response, he sounded defensive, which was unlike him as well.

He was holding back and she knew it. "Come on Rafe—there's no need to hide from me—I want the truth, and I want it now."

"Okay then, I will tell you if that's what you want," he responded with a bristle in his own voice. "One of our new board members, man by the name of Riggins, recommended Black Cat, and thinking it was good business, I contracted with them for security. Later, I started hearing things I didn't like about the company, so I ended the contract. My mistake was in not securing a new company. I've messed things up for your homecoming BJ, and I'm sick about it. Can you forgive me?"

Still cool, but at least understanding Rafe's mishandling of the situation, she forgave him.

61

By the end of the next day, the house was in livable condition again and ready for BJ's possessions. Bobbie Ann was in the bedroom when she called out, "Matt, BJ, somethin's missin' in here," pointing at the bed and nightstand. "It niggles in the back of my mind like a toothache that won't go away. Something should be sittin' right there."

She pointed at the empty spot on the dresser and gasped, "I know, it's the ivory shaft—Ben pulled it from a sinkhole not too long ago, that's what's missing! It was unusual, a heavily carved ivory shaft, a real long one, and perfectly intact. It was probably mastodon, with designs in a crosshatch pattern. It was different from anything we had found in the past. We thought maybe the Indians traded for it with another culture. I saw it just before the accident. Maybe he had it with him when the car crashed. We can ask Randy if they found anything..."

She stopped briefly, sucking in her breath and looking down at her feet. Matt and BJ discreetly said nothing. Then she continued, "He was excited about it, and was planning to take it to the RA Gray lab in Tallahassee for dating and analysis. It should go to the Museum of Florida History with the other pieces he donated from this land." At that, she stopped speaking and stood there exposed in her grief.

BJ put her arm around Bobbie Ann's shoulder, saying nothing. She knew Bobbie Ann was tough beneath the surface, as a career high school composition and creative writing teacher she'd had to be—her soft voice could quell even the most rebellious classroom, but this was a vulnerable woman she held.

Matt watched with interest and concern as BJ consoled Bobbie Ann. He had not known just how close Ben and Bobbie were until now— Ben was a private man and Bobbie Ann obviously knew how to be discreet. He knew Bobbie Ann was close to both Ben and his late wife, Nora, in the past, but it was evident their relationship had evolved into something far deeper than casual friendship.

Chapter 12

Randall Crum spoke to Matt later in the day telling him to keep watch on the women, saying, "There's no tellin' who's out there and there's lots of places to hide in those swamps. With y'all livin' down on the river in those dense woods, it'll be hard to keep watch. I'm deputizin' you, Walker. Get that gun I know you have, and keep it on you at all times. You know where I'm comin' from? Somethin's real wrong here, and I don't want either of those women hurt. You understand?"

Matt nodded, "We can't let them know I'm doing it in order to keep watch over them, or they *will* go off on their own without telling us. Deal?" the men shook hands on it, but as the sheriff drove away, he left Matt with a worried frown on his face.

Later that day, Matt watched BJ as she worked at the house, surprised at how little changed she was in spite of the years since he had last seen her. Still, there were subtle differences—how could there not be in two decades of living? Now, he found an aura of serenity about her at odds with the wildness of her wiry black and white hair, and laughter that seemed to erupt from her toes that he couldn't recall from their earlier time together. He found the lines around her eyes fascinating and the full lips still tempting and unsettling.

BJ was a striking woman: tall, almost stately in her bearing, and yet rawboned like a sapling. Her face, with the high cheekbones, square jaw, straight nose, and generous mouth of her Miccosukee ancestors, was surprisingly gentle. Her eyes, sometimes almost black, were deep smoky gray with golden lights that danced when she smiled. He found her arresting and discovered a deep need to protect her that had nothing to do with being a temporary deputy.

In spite of their secrecy, both women were aware of the agreement between Walker and Crum, and scoffed at the stereotypical male perception of female fragility and their perceived need for protection. Considering the events that followed, perhaps they should have taken their erstwhile protectors more seriously.

At Bobbie Ann's request, the highly respected shaman from the Miccosukee Tribe came in the afternoon and prayed all through the house, cleansing and blessing it in all four directions of the wind. With the elder's stern warning to keep the wild turkey wing fan over the door on their minds, they felt as though an evil spirit had been evicted from the house. To celebrate, BJ revved up the venerable Jeep Wagoneer, and drove them all down to the Riverside Restaurant on the St. Marks River for blackened grouper, huge salads and Key Lime pie. It was good to be home, BJ thought. She listened to the rhythms of the tide, inhaled the smell of the marshes and the Gulf just beyond and relaxed at last.

After dinner, they watched for manatees and saw the sun drop behind the marsh grasses; by the time they were finished, everybody was sleepy but nobody wanted to leave. They were discussing Ben and the wetlands restoration work when BJ's cell phone rang.

"Hello," she said, then paused, "oh, it's you, Randy. What did you find out?" She listened without speaking, an odd expression on her face. Finally, BJ caught her breath and closed her eyes, then quickly answered, glancing at the others, "Yes. Tomorrow at 10 am. Okay, we'll be there."

She snapped the phone shut, and dropped it on the table. Conversation ceased as all eyes turned to stare at BJ's suddenly pale face. BJ Hathaway wasn't an easy woman to rattle, but she looked shaken now. "It's Jake Collins; he's the one who's been living at the river house," she said. "He is out of prison for so called *good behavior*, but it was really due to prison overcrowding. He got out a couple of

64

months ago and wouldn't you know it, he headed straight back up here like this place was a magnet or something. Aren't we blessed?" she added sardonically.

To the stunned faces in front of her, Bobbie Ann spoke very carefully, "I'm not happy Jake Collins is out, but I'd rather know it than have you caught by surprise again. They should have built the prison on top of that pond scum. There's no kind of jail-time long enough for that one. Just knowin' that good for nothin' skunk has been creeping around Ben's place, sleepin' in his bed and trashing the river house makes me damned angry."

BJ nodded in agreement, rocking back and forth as fireflies blinked on and off in the deepening darkness of nightfall.

"Prisons all over are crowded to overflowing so they're letting criminals out that should stay for life, and Jake Collins is surely one of them," Bobbie Ann continued, still on her platform. "He always took advantage of Ben because Ben was too good to him. Ben even testified before the grand jury on Jake's behalf the first time he went to prison, and then when he got out, he let him work around the house off and on for years. Some repayment this is."

"I guess that explains how he knew where everything was and didn't have to break in. I can't believe the sheriff didn't know he was here," said BJ. "Aren't they supposed to be notified when somebody's let out of prison?"

Matt spoke without thinking, making the supreme blunder of all blunders, "Now *ladies*, Jake Collins is one bad number and we've got to be careful. I think we need to let Randy do his job, answer his questions when he asks them and stay out of his way. Beyond the mess he made at the river house, we don't know what Jake Collins is up to, but now, it could be revenge."

BJ bristled as he spoke, the fire in her eyes glittering at him, "Oh, get off it, Matt," she said, her voice harsh and rasping in anger. "That man desecrated my home and Ben's memory. I'll do whatever I have to do if the opportunity arises, and you know it. Don't try to stop me."

Bobbie Ann agreed with her saying, "We are not spring chickens, Matt Walker. Ain't nobody gonna' want us for our bodies—at least not mine," this, at BJ's lifted eyebrow, "so I doubt we are in any real physical danger. No, that man wants easy money, count on it."

Matt wasn't so sure. He'd heard the stories of Jake's infatuation with BJ as they were growing up, and he knew about the old feud over the land. This was brewing into something particularly nasty, and he feared the worst before it came to a head. No, he was not comfortable nor was he going to "get off it," especially since he was now officially an undercover agent working for the sheriff's department. Belatedly, he also realized he had some patching up to do.

"Look, I'm sorry I spoke like that," he said. "I'm worried to death about you, BJ, and you, too, Bobbie Ann. This man is clearly dangerous and a menace. We've all got to be careful."

Still offended, BJ turned a cold-shoulder in his direction. Watching them, Bobbie Ann saw the steel in his back stiffen in return and jumped into the fracas with both feet.

"Aw come on y'all, you've been together two days and you're already snapping like turtles. I never saw anybody for going at each other the way you two do. It's just like before isn't it—best friends one minute and worst enemies the next. Now, listen to auntie: it looks to me like if you'd go ahead and get together, and have sex, you could let off some of that built-up-steam, and the world would be a better place for it. We don't have time for you two to act like spoiled children."

Matt and BJ looked at her as one, their faces flushed in anger, but the words on their lips stopped in mid-sentence, amazed by what came out of her mouth.

"I mean it," said the normally mild-mannered Bobbie Ann Rice, slamming the table with the flat of her hand. "Either you get with it and enjoy life a little—maybe together—or cool off and let us all live in peace. I'm already tired of dealing with you two; besides, there's no reason for it. Life is short. Now, if you can behave, we've got serious business to discuss here."

Shocked into silence, neither said a word when the server came to check on them. Having overheard parts of their conversation, she started to speak, thought better of it, poured water all around, and left them alone. Their discussion disturbed her—the very idea of Robin with that man made her blood run cold. Had they but known what she knew, they might have saved themselves some time. She was aware her friend Robin was hanging out with Jake Collins, even though she had not personally seen him since his return. She could not imagine why Robin got herself mixed up with him unless it was drugs, and that was her best guess. She knew Robin was a good girl until she got hooked on meth, and started hanging out with older men like Jake Collins, but she kept what she knew to herself.

Chapter 13

The moon was high overhead by the time BJ dropped Bobbie Ann off and then drove Matt back to his car at the river house. A strange awkwardness arose between them, and they spoke little on the short drive down HWY 98 to Taylor's Run.

Deeply moved by the man sitting next to her—and she had been from the moment she heard his voice on the phone at Rafe Alford's office, she knew this was no time for a casual romance in spite of Bobbie Ann's urging. The trouble of it came down to the memories of their time together—memories that rushed in on her like a tsunami, and the avalanche of new emotions that were getting more confusing by the minute. Surely, they were too old for this kind of thing; the time for this kind of foolishness was long past. . .

Before he got out, Matt said, "BJ, what have I done to make you angry with me? Talk to me, please! Was it something I said?"

Ignoring him, she shook her head and ran up the steps, leaving him below, cursing as he walked to his truck. The look on his face stayed with her all that first night alone in the river house. She barely slept for fear of intrusion, hearing every creak the old house made, longing to open the windows, but afraid to do so. Above all, she longed for the man who lived next door.

Matt drove home angry, but when Chi greeted him, bushy tail wagging, his mood softened. His anger was gone by the time the dog came in from a brief run. "Well, at least you love me like I am, old boy. I don't know what that woman has against me, but I'm tired of it already.

Don't guess there's much I can do until she tells me. Meanwhile, I'm backing off that one. We have other things to do right now, like catch a rat." He ruffled the big shaggy red head and walked through the house. Satisfied all was safe, at least for that night, he went to sleep with BJ Hathaway on his mind.

When the phone rang the next morning BJ awoke still angry, feeling like she'd been on a four-day drunk. The pillow was damp from the tears she had shed before dropping into an exhausted sleep, thinking this was nothing like what she expected to find on her return to Florida. Groping around for her reading glasses on the nightstand, she found the phone and answered groggily, "Hello?"

"BJ, can you and Bobbie Ann meet me in Crawfordville about 10:00 this mornin'? Walker will be there, too," said Sheriff Crum. "A woman was spotted at the drug store at Wakulla Station trying to get antibiotic cream for a dog bite. I want y'all to look at the pictures so we'll all know her if we see her again."

The drive into Crawfordville was uncomfortable for BJ. Bobbie Ann was worried and when she was upset, she talked a blue streak. BJ was just the opposite—clamming up. Bobbie Ann went on and on, almost to the point of BJ's wanting to leave the car before she said something she'd regret.

When the silence from BJ's side of the car deepened, Bobbie Ann failed to notice as she continued sharing her concerns.

"Well, I do think you need to be more careful, BJ," said Bobbie Ann, rattling on non-stop. "I know you've lived in the desert by yourself and traveled all over the world alone, but there's been bad blood between you and Jake Collins ever since the high school prom. I remember that night like it was yesterday. You could become a target, too, you know."

BJ laughed at that, "Bad blood between Jake and me? You mean the fact he asked me on a date and I said no? For goodness sakes, Bobbie Ann, I was practically engaged to David Hathaway by then. I couldn't go to the prom with somebody else, could I?'

69

Bobbie Ann pursed her lips, "No, but we all know it was Jake who sprayed paint on David's car that night and wrote that nasty stuff on the windshield and you know it, too. Those kinds of memories don't go away in small towns like ours, now do they? By the way, don't try that flippant attitude with me old friend—it simply will not fly—I've known you since you were in pigtails, and I can tell when you're worried. Don't think that by clammin' up this will go away. You've *just got* to be careful. Real careful—do you *hear* me?"

Reluctantly, BJ had to agree. She had tried to block that horrible night out of her mind, but it popped up every now and then, and here it was again, coming out of Bobbie Ann's mouth. "Let's just deal with one thing at a time, okay? I don't want to think about the past," she said.

Bobbie Ann went on, ignoring her, "Seems to me like he's a bad dream that won't go away no matter what we do. Maybe somebody needs to off him instead of us all waitin' around for him to reappear every few years," she added.

Her vehemence finally got BJ's attention, shocking her as nothing else had. She turned to the tiny woman sitting next to her and point-blank asked, "Bobbie Ann, how long were you and Ben together, and why didn't you ever tell me?"

Suddenly, and with no warning, Bobbie Ann was crying hard. BJ pulled over and held her until she was coherent again.

"I'm sorry, I didn't mean to upset you, Bobbie Ann," she said. "You don't have to tell me anything until you are ready—if ever. Surely you know that."

The older woman pulled away and dried her eyes with a tissue pulled from her purse. "We didn't tell you because Ben and I wanted to keep our relationship private. I suppose we would have eventually moved in together, but I liked my space and he enjoyed his. As we got older, I could see he was going to need me, and I was ready to be there for him. Then he died. Gone—just like that!" she snapped her fingers. "I never got to hold him again; the last time I saw him alive he was in a coma. When I kissed him and told him how much I loved him, only his eyelashes flickered—no more movement than that. I have to believe he heard me and that was his reply. You will never know how hard that was."

BJ pulled back onto the road; they were silent until Bobbie Ann spoke so quietly that she had to lean over to hear her. "I don't want you to miss out on the happiness Matt Walker can give you, BJ. I don't want you to go through what I have. I loved Ben Taylor all the years I knew him, and only had him to myself near the end."

"Bobbie Ann," she replied, "I'm not sure I'm the marrying kind now. I did that once, and it was too hard to get out. I still have the emotional scars to prove it. Now that I understand where you are coming from, it will help. I just need you to back off a little and let us work through all of this other stuff before we get into relationships, okay?"

Bobbie Ann sniffed again, "Did I say anything about marriage?"

Stunned yet again by the prim and proper Bobbie Ann Rice, BJ found herself at a loss for words. A truce declared, both women were dry-eyed when they reached the sheriff's office, ready to confront whatever he had for them.

They were early, getting there before the sheriff, but when he came in, he was all business, showing them the photos taken of the woman shoplifting along with her legitimate purchases.

While not perfect, the photos showed a youngish woman, darkly tanned with streaked blond hair, dropping several containers into her bag while she shopped.

"I'll bet you anything Jake Collins is shackin' up with that woman, and she's doin' his business for him," said the sheriff, lodging a fresh plug of tobacco in his mouth.

BJ nodded and said, "Did anybody see what kind of car she was driving?"

He replied with, "Yeah, blue two-door coup, American...checked out under the name of Robin Wilson. Turns out, she graduated from Leon High School in Tallahassee, class of '75. Pharmacist said she came

71

in yesterday. Said she's had lots of colds just lately. Anyway, she got some antibiotic ointment and left. After she left, they were missing several boxes of cold medicine, just like a couple of days ago. We're on the lookout for her now."

They rose to leave with the sheriff walking them out to the car. "You get that dog yet, missy?"

"No, not yet," she replied, just a little irritated with him. "I haven't had time to get down to the animal shelter, but I will when I can."

"You'd better. A big, bad dog is a good deterrent for men like Collins." He watched them drive away, a concerned look on his face. Turning, he spat dark brown tobacco juice on the ground and yelled for Rusty. "Get in here, Rusty and tell me what you got on Jake Collins, and it better be good."

* * *

BJ felt awkward and bumbling as she walked into Myra Jean's beside the petite Bobbie Ann. She could see their reflections in the double door, and gave herself a stark appraisal. The lifestyle on the river suited her and she was adapting fast, in spite of the intruder. Tall and slender, she now wore T-shirts and jeans or shorts every day. She hadn't worn pantyhose in several weeks, and could go days without a speck of makeup on her face. Her nails, though nicely trimmed were unpolished. Her hair, bound in a long plait; well, that was a problem and she knew it. "I wonder what Matt…"

"Hello in there…knock-knock, is anybody home?" Bobbie Ann said. Trying to get her attention she spoke again, saying, "Where are you, girl? Have I got to carry you to the table myself or can you walk and talk at the same time?"

That got her and she responded, saying. "No. Oh, I'm sorry, Bobbie Ann, I was just thinking about Ben and the river house."

"I'll bet you were! It was Matt's name you were mumbling, Honey Chile'. You okay in there?" Bobbie Ann's far-seeing eyes peered up into BJ's, probably seeing far more than BJ wanted her too.

72

Embarrassed, BJ said, "I did? Oh, crap, I'm sorry; I'm just distracted, that's all."

"I'll say," said Bobbie Ann. "Brighten up or I won't buy your lunch."

BJ laughed as they found a table and ordered the house special—an all-beef cheeseburger with fries topped off with Coca-Cola. It was delicious, but she knew it wouldn't do to eat like that too often.

Her mood had softened considerably since the visit with Randy Crum. Maybe it wouldn't be so bad after all if they already knew who Jake's accomplice was. They would catch the culprit, put him behind bars again for breaking his parole and everything else; get Robin into treatment, and all would be well. She could then focus on what she had come to do—continue the work of restoring the marshlands along the river. Still, Jake's name came up again in spite of everything she tried to do.

"Jake's not stupid, Bobbie Ann, he's just crooked—twisted for some reason," BJ said. "He could have a degree in archeology if he had cared to try, which he didn't. Ben saw his potential and did everything he could for him when he was a kid. He even paid his tuition at Florida State a couple of semesters until he got kicked out for selling marijuana on campus. Still, I don't understand it—this is Jake's homeland. It's where his roots are, and it should mean everything to him."

"I know that, but I've seen what he does to sites, and it's desecration to be sure," Bobbie Ann replied. "When he gets in there, he's not interested in anything but what he can sell, and tears everything apart in the search. Looks like a prehistoric giant armadillo got in there and tore holes into the ground. The stuff he ruined is legendary and difficult to forgive. The thing is, he has a nose for it—he can sense quality in artifacts and antiquities, but he cares little for them beyond the money he gets at the point of sale."

Bobbie Ann nodded to herself and continued, "Jake knew Ben had some nice pieces down at the river, and he also knew he had already donated a fair amount to the Museum of Florida History. He's probably trying to make sure he gets the rest it. Feels entitled to it, he does."

The women planned a shopping trip into Tallahassee the next week, and then Bobbie Ann proposed a trip down to the blueberry patch on the Wacissa River, saying they needed to keep some normalcy in their lives even if Jake Collins was on the loose.

Chapter 14

The next day, BJ took Bobbie Ann's boat out on the river and followed it all the way to its confluence with the Wakulla and on to the Gulf of Mexico. The day was hot from the time the sun came up. As she made her way down the river, a breeze from the Gulf wafted up the channel, keeping most of the insects at bay. She delighted in the clear water and air, laughing at an osprey as it scolded her from high above.

The sun was setting when she docked the boat late that afternoon. Too tired to eat, she worked listlessly at her computer catching up on correspondence with her friends out in New Mexico. Analinda was already hinting at a Florida vacation if it could include something in the Keys. BJ smiled and shook her head as she shut down the computer. Did the woman have *any* idea how far from the Keys BJ now lived?

Restless, she walked around the deck to see if Matt was home. He'd been out on another research trip and left Chi with her. She thought he might be back, but no, the house was dark and his carport was empty. She walked back around the house to face the river, watching the eagles fish. Something felt wrong, but she couldn't put her finger on it.

Martha circled anxiously around her legs, complaining of neglect. She laughed as the cat jumped up in front of her at the sink, trying to bat the water as she washed her hands. She fed the cat, took a shower, scrambled some eggs and ate them thoughtfully, barely tasting the food. When she climbed into bed after setting the new alarm system, the long day out on the water finally took its toll. The book she was reading fell to the floor as deep sleep overtook her.

* * *

After clearing the undergrowth between the houses, their small community kept watch on the river and one another, but it took some getting used to. One of the reasons folk lived in places like that was for the privacy, but some compromises were necessary under the circumstances. As a result, they grew closer.

BJ's house was in the middle, with quiet ceiling fans on the screened porch upstairs, and the breezeway below, which was also screened-in, so they met there often in the evenings for coffee and conversation when the weather permitted.

They gathered earlier than usual that afternoon, seeking sanctuary before the mosquitoes began feeding at twilight. BJ's lavender bug light was active, frequent smacks and pops keeping an irregular backbeat to the conversation as they watched the sun set over the marsh grass. The moon, coming into her fullness showed big, golden, and opulent. The night was warm and sultry with barely any breeze. Out of habit, they rocked as one, watching the moonrise over the river. All three enjoyed the ritual with Ben and Nora in the past. Their conversation had a pattern to it, both relaxing and comforting in its regularity—it was completely natural.

BJ looked up as the moon topped the moss-laden oak trees. Pointing at the translucent wings beating in the treetops in front of the golden orb, she said, "Look, the fairies are dancing before the Moon Goddess tonight."

She was absorbed in the fairy dance—caring not that perhaps they were fireflies magnified by the moon's fullness. To her, in that moment of fantasy, they were fairies, called from their haunts to perform a ritual older than memory.

Matt watched her joy with pleasure. BJ's endless fascination with nature intrigued him, and often opened his own practical eyes to other worlds existing within the one he thought he could see.

76

Bobbie Ann saw him watching the other woman, still praying something would come of the attraction this time around. They needed one another, she was sure of it. The thought of needing someone caused her heart to constrict—she missed Ben more than ever.

As he left, Matt leaned into BJ briefly and said, "Thank you for a wonderful evening."

Without thinking, she responded warmly and kissed him—a fairy-light kiss so fleeting he barely felt it, then drew back, watching his flashlight flicker as he escorted Bobbie Ann home.

"Don't forget to pick me up in the morning, Bobbie Ann," she called. "I will have coffee ready and waiting. I can't wait to get my hands on those ripe blueberries! My buckets are already at the door."

Laughing, Matt and Bobbie Ann made their way to her place. On the way, she queried him gently about his feelings for BJ. Failing to resist her interrogation technique, he told her exactly how he felt.

"It's not as though I haven't had other relationships since we were together—some of them serious, but it's different with BJ. She's not like anyone I've ever known before or since, and the years apart have made her more appealing than ever. I feel like a lovesick puppy, but I don't think she sees me as anything beyond an old friend. It's driving me crazy!"

Bobbie Ann watched him carefully as he spoke, hearing the agony in his voice. Again, she wished she were younger—about ten or fifteen years might do it. But no, she thought again, BJ is his love, and somehow, BJ's got to get beyond her own reservations and fully open her heart to him.

* * *

BJ struggled to sleep that night—latent asthma had indeed stirred in the swampy wilderness. The products at her disposal this time around were more effective, but still, the inhaler always revved her up and made it harder to fall asleep. After what seemed like hours trying to drift off, she was finally sinking into oblivion when she heard rustling noises in the side yard. The room brightened when the security light came on and she groaned, turning over to turn on the bedside lamp, thinking, "It's probably those darned raccoons after the garbage cans again."

Peering out over the deck railing, she couldn't see anything, so she re-set the flood lights to stay on just in case it was the raccoons on a raid, and padded back to bed. She was nearly asleep when she heard noises again, but this time the room was dark. She flipped the switch on her bedside lamp—nothing happened.

Alarmed, she got out of bed, grabbed the old chenille robe she'd found hanging in the closet—one of Nora's, and shrugged into it. Slowly, armed with the crowbar she kept by the bed, she walked from window to window.

Finally, against her better judgment and every voice of caution she had ever heard in her entire life, she crept around the side of the house and down the back steps, following the noises coming from the garden. By this time, she was certain it wasn't a bear—she kept no food in the garbage cans for them to raid, and surely a raccoon would have been on its way by now...opossum? The trashcans were upright—undisturbed; she wondered what happened to the security lights. What was out there?

What she found was comically ludicrous: Jake Collins was digging in the old sawdust pile in her yard!

Sudden raging anger overcame wisdom. She stormed at him, pink robe flapping around her legs, unbound hair wild. Acting out of long pent-up anger and fury, she raised the crowbar to strike him dead.

"Jake Collins," she said, hesitating, arm in mid-air, "Just what do you think you are doing, digging in *my* backyard? Get out!"

He looked up calmly as if he dug in backyards every night of the year, "Why, BJ, I didn't think you was home. I'm just lookin' for some personal property my great-granddaddy hid in this ole' sawdust pile way back when."

"Are you crazy, Jake? There's nothing in this backyard that belongs to you—somebody would have found it by now if there were.

This is my land and my house and you have no right to be here," she said, and again approached him, crowbar in hand, yelling, "Now get!"

He laughed softly at her—she had lost the element of surprise, and before she could move close enough to strike him, he grabbed the bar out of her hand and drew back as if to hit *her* with it. She cringed and when he saw it, he laughed again, picked her up easily with one arm, and then dropped her onto a lawn chair. "Now you just stay there Missy, while I finish this little job, and then we'll settle some old business that's been a'festerin' for too long between you and me."

Finally, regretting her lack of wisdom and foul temper, she clutched the robe close to her chest, realizing her vulnerability. Instinctively, she knew better than to scream—it was highly unlikely anyone would hear her anyway, considering the distance between the houses. Jake could easily kill her before help arrived. She sat quietly, afraid to breathe for fear of angering him, angry with herself for her foolishness.

Perspiring in the warm, moist night air, she sat rooted to the chair watching him poke around in the dense sawdust. She hated seeing it defiled like that—that pile was leftover from the timber operations earlier in the century, and something she and Ben had left for future exploration. Now she saw first-hand the degradation Bobbie Ann had described to her and felt yet another flash of anger. She watched him feverishly dig around until he finally hit something metallic. Clink! Curious, she watched as he pulled up a rusted, black box, dancing a jig as he exclaimed in a stage whisper,

"Ye-hi! It's still here. Well, ain't this my day! Ain't you jealous? There was this here val-u-able box sittin' in the ground all this time that you and your precious Ben knew nothing about!"

He giggled at her silence in a high, artificial-sounding voice, saying, "You was a 'diggin' all around this ole' pile of sawdust, but never *in* it. This box ain't yours, neither—finders keepers, I say," dusting the box with reverence as he spoke. "Inside this lil-ole thing are the deeds to this land you're squattin' on."

She watched as he worked at the latch, realizing their little community had relaxed too much in the past few months. Seeing or hearing nothing from him, they thought Collins had gone into hiding, probably leaving the area. As a result, they had grown careless. However, the danger was standing in front of her alive and well, and she was alone with him in the dark of night.

BJ kept quiet, trying to shrink into the lawn chair. Jake was as reliable as a snake, she thought, and just as sneaky, and she had no intention of shaking his rattles if she could help it. He could have what was in the box for all she cared, but somehow she figured that wasn't all he was after.

He stepped out of the flowerbed, compressing the newly-planted flowers already wilting on the grass, and stared at her for a few minutes. When he spoke, it was to say, "You saved me havin' to wake you up to conclude this little business between you and me, Old Girl. Don't worry, I ain't gonna rape you, at least not now. I got me some young pussy and don't need no shriveled up bitty like you. Get your keys, Ms. Hathaway, we're goin' for a ride. You don't think I'm goin' to leave you here to go runnin' off to Matt Walker, do you?"

At her look, he giggled, pulling her up from the chair and holding her close. She gagged at his foul breath as he spoke, "Shit, don't you know everybody and their house cat knows about you and him? I been watchin' y'all for months now. Ain't you too old to be playin' them kind of games?"

She tried to draw back, saying, "There's nothing…" but he grabbed her, leering, "Well, after I'm done, he won't want nothin' more out of you and that's for certain." He paused and added, "What's the matter, cat got your tongue, Old Girl? Go on now, get me them keys. "

She knew bone-chilling fear as she made for the steps, praying that just maybe she'd live through the night.

Carrying the box and the crowbar, he followed her as she felt her way up the steps and into the dark house to get the keys, and then back down the stairs. Gripping her arm in a bruising hold at the bottom, Jake dragged her into the laundry room. There, he trussed her up with some old clothesline, stuffed a washrag in her mouth, and forced her into the backseat of the Wagoneer.

Throwing a freshly laundered sheet on top of her he said, "That ought to take care of you, Betsy Jane Hathaway. Now you just take a little nap. We'll talk after a while, maybe have a little fun. Depends on how good you are."

Jake backed the heavy car out and crept up the drive to the highway without the lights on. Once he hit HWY 98, he gunned the engine and they roared down the highway. Fear mixed with nausea as BJ tried to keep from rolling into the floor behind the front seat. Throbbing pain in her head matched every beat of her heart.

* * *

Bobbie Ann arrived at BJ's at daybreak and was surprised to find the Wagoneer gone. She parked her car under the house from long habit, and carefully approached the central stairs with caution. All was quiet and dark; the door to the downstairs entry by the laundry was open. At the top, Martha crouched just inside the door, meowing desperately. Slowly, she walked up the stairs, calling BJ's name.

"BJ, I'm here," she called. "Where's my coffee?"

Getting no answer, she grew even more cautious. There was little to indicate anything was awry other than the old car's absence, but of course, BJ could have left it at Miner's Garage the day before, and gotten a ride home. Still, the open doors both downstairs and upstairs bothered her. Why hadn't Martha ventured downstairs through the open door? Something was wrong and everything inside her pulsated with prescient knowledge.

Pushing the door open to sidestep a frantic Martha, she saw BJ's tan leather purse lying open on the counter where she always laid it. Beside it was her asthma inhaler.

"Where's your mama, Little Cat?" she asked, scooping Martha up in her arms. The cat struggled and meowed as though she was trying to speak, but could not make herself understood. She did a better job

81

than she knew—by that time, Bobbie Ann knew something was terribly wrong at Taylor's Run. Slowly, she walked toward the bedroom.

"BJ, are you okay?" she called again. Silence. She grabbed her cell phone and dialed 911.

"This is 911, what is your location?" said the operator. Quickly, Bobbie Ann told the operator where she was and that BJ was gone. "We don't normally post missing persons until 24 hours have passed, ma'am," said the polite voice on the other end.

"Listen, I'm Bobbie Ann Rice. It's BJ Hathaway we're talkin' about here, and I suspect foul play," she said with an unnatural force in her soft voice. "You get Randall Crum and tell him we need help at Taylor's Run, NOW!" Then she called Matt, who got the message loud and clear with no prompting. "I'm on my way," he said.

She was waiting outside when Matt skidded into the yard, and just after him, Sheriff Randall Crum with half a dozen deputies—lights blazing, sirens roaring. Their old friend Randy was brusque in his questioning, friendship put aside for the moment, "What do you mean you went into the house?" he yelled at Bobbie Ann. "What the hell were you thinking, goin' in there like that, woman?" Then, simmering down to a mere boil, "Well, tell me about it."

Chapter 15

BJ lay on the hard back seat, sweating in the steamy heat, sickened by the foul smell emitting from a ranting Collins. He fumed at members of her family, school, Ben Taylor, Bobbie Ann, Matt Walker and more, accusing them of being upstarts and carpetbaggers. It seemed as though few in their small community escaped his wrath. That his captive was unable to talk back gave him a thrill. He drove too fast, using the dark road like a speedway.

BJ listened to his rant—she had to, but found herself unable to think beyond fear and discomfort.

Finally, running out of venom, Collins began to have second thoughts about what he had done. He meant to find the black metal box, but the kidnapping had taken him by whim without thought of consequence, as most things did.

He was making for the trailer in the swamp, even though he knew Robin would be angry with him for bringing the woman to their hideout. However, the more he thought about it, the more he felt he was in a power position, and it went to his head. To hell with Robin—he finally had the high and mighty BJ Hathaway in his possession, and he meant to use her hard. Then he looked down at the box by his side. If it contained what he hoped for, he wouldn't need BJ or Robin. With a maniacal giggle, he turned sharply off the highway, slinging BJ against the door handle as he rammed the tough old car over deep ruts and pushed into the swamp.

BJ, flung from one side to the other as the car careened on the logging track, felt like a rag doll. Nausea struck and she threw up, adding the sour smell of vomit to the man's perspiration and the chemical odors that permeated the car.

The road got rougher in the dense jungle, and the heavy station wagon scraped roots and dug into ruts, but it did little to slow Jake's bone-jarring mad drive. When they finally came to a stop, he got out of the car, leaving the door open. He hoped Robin was gone. Without her, he could deal with BJ as he wanted, but it turned out Robin was still there.

Outside in the car, still trussed up, hot and cramped, BJ welcomed the cooler air until opportunistic mosquitoes began their unmerciful torture, stinging her exposed feet and ankles, face and hands.

She lay still, trying to hear Jake's movements, hoping he had forgotten her. When she finally heard voices—Jake's and a woman, they were arguing.

"If you had to take a captive, why couldn't you have found some other way to bring her, like on that damned boat you use to deliver your junk or something? Now we have a stolen car for that big bad Sheriff to find, and *she's* a smart cookie who will figure out what's going on down here. Why *did* you bring her here? Where you gonna put her?" Then petulantly, "This place is supposed to be a secret, and it has been up till now. Somebody's gonna' come lookin' for her, you damned idiot."

"I know. I'm not stupid, Robin," he said, angry and ready to strike out at her for speaking to him that way. "I needed to prove something, but now I've got her here, I gotta do something with her."

BJ lay still, unable to sit up and so thirsty her tongue stuck to the roof of her mouth. Coherent thought escaped her, crowded out by flies, mosquitoes and deadly heat. She prayed somebody would think about her before the sun rose, and the truly intense heat of the day began. Jake and Robin were quiet for a while, and she guessed Jake knew how to calm the woman down, because before long, she could hear groaning, and finally, Jake's climax. Then it stopped. Their talk became desultory and subdued. She could smell something—it was odd and strangely familiar, not unlike the smell she had noted on Jake. She dozed off, awakening again to the sounds of sex in the trailer. She was profoundly grateful to be outside in the car at that point, but her bound arms were on fire and she desperately needed to empty her bladder. Finally, she drifted off to sleep again, finding comfort in the gentle hoot of an owl nearby.

* * *

Jake cursed under his breath, pushing away from Robin. It was too hot to stay close together in the claustrophobic trailer during the day, so he moved to the sofa, finding refuge in sleep. When he woke, stiff from sleeping with his knees bent to his chest, he stumbled into the bedroom. Robin lay where he left her, still in the camp bed, naked, her legs splayed open, hands limp on the rumpled sheets, her head hanging half-off the tiny bed. Flies buzzed around the drool from her open mouth and the waxen sickly pallor of her flesh.

"Hey, Robin, wake up," he whispered. "I need you to bandage my leg." Feeling fresh blood streaming from the wound where the festering dog bite had reopened, he pushed her over so he could lie down. Instead of warm, vital flesh, he discovered a cold resistant body.

"Oh, shit," he said to himself, completely without remorse for the body lying in the bed, angry at the inconvenience her demise caused. "What am I going to do now?" he thought, without guilt or conscience.

He sat next to the body for a while, trying to think. Finally, he got up and splashed some peroxide on his wound. Then, cursing under his breath, pulled several big black plastic trash bags out from under the kitchen sink. Quickly, he tripled the bags, wrapped the body in the top sheet, then forced the stiffening body inside and dragged it to the sofa.

That ought to hold her until I figure out what to do. I gotta' get some sleep, he said to himself, and crawled into the bed. He awoke to the sticky wet heat of a hot, humid North Florida day, and made his plans to dispose of the body after dark. He half-carried, half-dragged it down the steps and out to the Wagoneer.

85

Beyond tears now, BJ heard him struggling out of the trailer. When he lifted the bag to push it through the rear door, she saw a stiff leg break through the plastic, and the body's thud when it fell into the space behind her. She lay quiet, fearful of making a sound that would remind the man she was still there. In spite of herself, she inhaled the chemical odors wafting from the trailer, and those of rapidly decomposing flesh. Revolted, she gagged and vomited again into the rag, choking on her own phlegm.

* * *

Sheriff Randall Crum walked around the river house like a panther on the prowl. "Somebody's been in here and that's a fact. I would bet you a dime to a dollar it was Jake Collins," he growled. "Matt, you and Bobbie Ann go over to her place and stay out of my way. I'll call you when I know something."

At signs of protest from Bobbie Ann he said, "I mean it Bobbie Ann Rice. Will you stay out of my way for now? If I need anything from you, I will call you. Now, will you do as I say? *Will you?*" When she reluctantly nodded, he looked at Matt Walker and said, "I need your help, Walker. I need you to stay with Bobbie Ann, and do not let her out of your sight. Do that for me. Okay?" He had a wad of chewing tobacco stuffed in the side of his mouth and the gray eyes beneath the broad-brimmed hat were dark with anger.

She disliked the powerless feeling, but for once, Bobbie Ann did as she was told. She and Walker sat on her covered deck under the ceiling fan all morning, eyes focused on BJ's house, watching as the sheriff's deputies hung yellow crime scene tape and began the investigation.

Chapter 16

As the news leaked out, television trucks mounted with massive satellite dishes circled the tiny community, holding it ransom, hungry for news. Reporters with tiny handheld mics clustered at BJ's house, hovering near the yellow tape like bees drawn to a honeycomb. Bobbie Ann and Matt felt like hostages themselves as they camped out at her place waiting for news. Finally, the sheriff stationed a deputy in her driveway to keep the reporters away. As it was, the watchers had a spectacular view of the law enforcement investigation and the press at work, but felt rising panic when there was no news of BJ.

Gradually, neighbors from St. Marks, Crawfordville and on to Panacea braved the press brigade to gather at Bobbie Ann's house. Friends brought food and comfort with them, but when everyone left for home at nightfall, Bobbie Ann and Matt kept their vigil. The birds were quiet that night. For once, the mullet were still, and the gators kept to their dens.

It was late when Sheriff Crum dropped by the house. "Well, folks, it's foul play, we know that much. Looks like Jake was diggin' out back of BJ's house for some ungodly reason—probably for artifacts, and she must have surprised him. We found Ben's boat further down the river with some digging tools and brushes in it, but where he's taken her we don't know at this time. We think he must have a hideout somewhere back in those swamps." He saw Matt flinch, but the words were out, and he couldn't take them back.

His cell phone rang and the sheriff nodded into it, grunting, "I gotta go. We're doin' everything we can to find her. Y'all call me if you hear anything."

Bobbie Ann and Matt kept an anxious watch all night as helicopters covered every inch of the area, their searchlights illuminating the landscape like huge fireflies.

"You know, I have known BJ since she was in 1st grade," said Bobbie Ann. "She was over at the old Woodville School when I was a new teacher. I hadn't started my writing yet. We met over a yellow crayon she wanted to color a silly duck, and only yellow would do. I've been fond of her ever since. I'm so afraid she's hurt or having an asthma attack somewhere without her medicine."

"Or dead," thought Matt, but he refused to say it aloud. He felt utterly powerless and frustrated beyond endurance, but the sheriff was very clear in his instructions: watch Bobbie Ann. He fingered the gun in his pocket with a grim expression on his face; he would do his duty by her, but what he really wanted was to be part of the action. He wanted to see Jake Collins dead.

Daybreak brought no real news, and after Matt made coffee, they walked over to see if there was any news. There they found police tape blocked their way as well as that of the press camped out along the edge of the driveway. Officers who were their friends and neighbors in normal times presented stern, sad faces. Without good news to tell, they refused to talk about the case at all, referring friends and press alike to the Sheriff, who was officially unavailable. Once they were recognized, members of the press leapt into action, laying siege on them with camcorders picking up every expression. Bobbie Ann and Matt gave brief statements, and then left under escort, feeling overwhelmed, frustrated and useless. They retreated to Bobbie Ann's place again, seeking sanctuary from the madness that had come into their lives. Even there they knew the intrusion as a deep, emotional enemy. Both knew life would be agony until they knew what had happened to BJ.

Chapter 17

Jake woke up slowly. His wound, clotted to the sheets, tore when he stretched. Cursing, he struggled out of the cramped bed and looked around for Robin. It was then that he remembered Robin was no longer there to tend to his needs. Perhaps there was another he could coerce into helping...

Gasping in pain from the infected dog bite, he stumbled out to the Wagoneer, where he found the woman asleep. At first, he thought she was dead, too, but was relieved when she opened frightened eyes and searched his face.

"I ain't goin' to hurt you, if you behave," he said. "In fact, you be a real good girl, I'll untie you and take that rag out of your mouth and let you go pee. How's about that for starters?" At her startled expression, he couldn't resist adding, "Then we might have a little fun."

He cackled at that, and spreading his arms wide, said, "Don't you try to run old girl. Look around you—there ain't nowhere for you to go."

She nodded, clueless as to the motives behind anything Jake did, and far too anxious to pee to think about what he called *fun*. He was a stranger now, not the kid she played with and ran from in the summers. She found the tiny bathroom with the greatest relief in memory, thinking the fact that she had held her water was a major miracle. Finally relieved, she stood up and stretched, washed her hands and face, taking her time to delay going back to Jake. She twisted and wound her hair, then knotted it, and immediately felt cooler.

As the trailer's odoriferous and fetid air penetrated her senses, she knew it was time to go back to Jake. Memories from the night before flooded her mind as she fumbled her way in the semi-dark, but she pushed them away. She needed every ounce of brainpower she possessed to find a way out of this predicament.

Sweating, and sickened by the miasma of smells she encountered inside, BJ longed to take her robe off. She dared not, Jake's comment about 'having a little fun,' lingering in her mind. When she came out of the minuscule bathroom, he was waiting for her. She found him sitting on the soiled sofa, trying to doctor the dog bite with any ideas of *fun* abandoned to his wound.

"Since you are here, Ms. BJ," he said in a cynical tone of voice, "maybe you could help me with this little dog bite I got here."

Nodding, she walked over to him, trying not to gag again, and carefully looked at the wound. It was swollen, red and purple; thick, greenish yellow puss oozed from under the edges of the moist scab. "Have you got hydrogen peroxide?" she asked.

He told her to look in the cupboard and when she opened the door, boxes of cold medicine fell out—that and other strange ingredients. Then it dawned on her what he was doing and what the odor meant, too.

She turned around and with more surprise than wisdom said, "So that's where the strange smell comes from, and I'll bet the die-back, too! You're cooking drugs down here, aren't you?" She regretted the words the minute they came from her mouth, but it was too late.

His eyes darkened with rage. Snarling, he lunged for her, but fell back, pain from the bite stopping him for the moment. "You keep your eyes, ears and mouth shut, you nosy bitty, and you *may* live through this. I haven't decided. What I do down here is my business, you hear me?"

Propelled by the volcanic anger in his voice, she nodded and cautiously took the peroxide, cotton balls, and ointment she found to the man. The bite was bleeding now, and Jake's face was white from the pain that streaked up and down his leg. Very gently, she tore the cotton, cleaned the nasty wound, and then spread antibiotic ointment on it.

Carefully, she bandaged the leg and backed away from him against the open door, afraid of what he might do next, and too afraid to try to escape.

He sat there for a long time, ignoring her, trying to think. Things had been going well since he got out of prison, but now the smell of leg irons was in his nostrils again. Robin was dead and decomposing in the back of the Wagoneer. Now he had BJ on his hands and he didn't know what to do with her. Stupid, that's what it was, just plain stupid. Angry, confused and miserable, he lay back on the sofa, eyes pressed shut.

Tired and too angry to think straight, Jake drifted off to sleep, leaving BJ alone with her thoughts. She watched him for a while, trying to find traces of the troubled boy she knew as a child, but all she could find was a man ravaged by hate.

She stood in the open doorway of the trailer, hoping for a light breeze. Watching the cypress swamp soothed her. Strangely, she experienced a strange sense of companionship, almost as though the trees were trying to reassure her. Trying to formulate an escape plan, she noticed the blue, two-door compact car parked in the back. That was the car from the pharmacy photos! If only Randall knew… She glanced around—she knew Jake still had her keys, but where were the keys to the little car?

The trailer sat on a gently mounded sand hill, but beyond it was the dark creek stained the color of tea from acidic cypress tree tannin, its edges bumpy with rusty-looking cypress knees. Several old trees stretched high in the sky trying to find the sun, their leaves and needles pale and sickly looking. Their branches met overhead, creating a dark tunnel over the creek that seemed to end in a cove near where the mound rose from the ground. BJ wondered if the mound was a midden—an Indian burial mound. Something about it looked vaguely familiar: she and Ben had taken the boat out on the river to look for old trees, and something about this place made her think of that day.

Memories flooded her mind as she stared at her surroundings, changing the tenor of what she could see now. Vividly, she remembered the day that changed the direction of her life.

They were in the watery, canopied tunnel that was Blackwater Creek when she felt almost as though the water called to her. It was a day of mystery compounded when Ben said, "That's it, Girl. Can you see it?" She remembered looking up to see hundreds of young trees, but then finally, her eyes focused on what was there—a cypress tree so wide she could hardly see its sides, so tall it reached far into the sky above all the other trees. "It's the last of the giant cypress trees in this region!" Ben said.

She climbed up the bank, and pushed through the undergrowth until she reached the ancient tree. There, she felt drawn to lean into that rough, stringy bark—to be a part of it. When she made her way back down to the boat, she knew she'd fight to keep that tangled wild place intact, and to protect that tree and the others around it. That day and that feeling were vivid to her now, and it seemed as though everything Jake Collins was doing conspired to keep her from success. Thoughts of passivity and fear fled from her. She had to escape.

Glancing back at Jake, she could see her keys just under his right hip, lying on the sofa, probably where they landed the night before. No, that wasn't going to be the way she got away from him, she thought to herself, but newly invigorated, she watched and planned, thinking hard. She realized they were many, many miles from the nearest paved road, having crossed several cattle grates and a number of switchbacks until Jake found the rough track that led them here. Had Ben's Jon boat been wedged among the cypress knees, it would have been simpler to affect an escape, but there was no boat.

By now, she mused, Bobbie Ann should have discovered she was missing and sounded the alarm. It was a given that Sheriff Crum would have every deputy on the force looking for her, but again, hope began to slide away. Present reality said she was deep in the Blackwater Swamp, and alone with Jake Collins. He was asleep in the trailer and seemed harmless for the moment, but awake, he was volatile, and she was realistic enough to be very afraid.

The sun rose high overhead and heat shimmered over the water— even dragonflies flew in slow droning patterns. It was hard to breathe, especially with the intensity of the odors coming out of the trailer. The strange scent in her own hair and the damp nightclothes she wore smelled so strong it caused her stomach to turn. An asthmatic rattle stirred deep in her chest, but she tried to keep her mind off it, thinking again of escape. Robin's keys were surely in the trailer, but going back inside was to risk waking the sleeping bear within.

She looked at her old blue and white Wagoneer and then back at Jake, wondering again how to get her keys away from him. The rugged car Ben had taken such pride in for so many years was mud-splashed, scraped and scratched from the wild ride they had taken during the night, and now dusted over with powdery white sand. One of the tires was low and the muffler was hanging loose; had she not known it was hers, she would never have recognized it.

Finally, too hot and tired of standing, she sat on the top step, untied the pink wrap and tried to fan herself while the man inside slept on. The dense jungle looked impenetrable and mysterious, and had she been there for any other reason, it would have given her great pleasure. Instead, her sense of direction compromised, she experienced an inner sense of warning that kept her from trying to run. She now knew what it was like to be a captive with no ropes—intimidation was powerful.

Young cypress trees clustered around their elders, creating a landscape beneath which very little seemed to grow but ferns and knobby cypress knees. A snowy white egret on tall, skinny black legs poked around in the shallow water nearby. A small green heron fished at the water's edge. Jake slept on.

Drowsy, she leaned against the flimsy trailer doorframe until she heard the loud drone of helicopters approaching. There were two of them, both moving slowly overhead and without thinking, she jumped up, shouting and waving, the pink robe flapping around her like bird's wings, crying out, "Help! Help me, please help me!"

Jake heard the helicopters, too, and as the cry for help left her mouth, he rose from the sofa and hit her in the back of the head. Darkness closed around her and she fell limp as a rag doll, rolling down the steps. It was too late to run.

93

Jake dragged her into the trailer. He pulled the door shut and threw her unconscious body on the bed with the soiled sheets. Crouching by the window, he watched as the helicopters circled around and around the swamp. When they finally left, he knew he had to take action, get rid of the woman and dispose of Robin's body. Surely, they hadn't seen the trailer under the big magnolia tree. He had camouflage screening over the top, but they might have seen the woman in her flapping pink bathrobe. One thing he knew for sure—there was no time to waste; he had to clear out of North Florida. Maybe he would head down to Eustis or even further south to the Everglades. Once there, he could carry on the time-honored Florida tradition of hiding in swamps so thick only the most desperate had the courage to navigate them.

He had come up with a tentative plan that he now put into action. Going out to the Wagoneer, he pulled the black bag that held his dead girlfriend out of the back and dragged it into the trailer, dumping it in the kitchenette without ceremony. Then he took BJ, who was regaining consciousness and beginning to moan, and dragged her, unresisting, to the Wagoneer. There, he stuffed her into the back where Robin's body had been, and slammed the door.

Cursing with pain, he hobbled back to the trailer and grabbed the chemicals he used to cook meth, sloshing them inside, coating every surface with the mix of highly flammable liquids. He took the black box from BJ's sawdust pile, the prized ivory shaft, and the treasured Bolen period projectile points from Ben's place. Working feverishly, he stuffed everything into a pillowcase, pushed several wads of cash into his pockets, took Robin's credit cards and the money in her purse, the prepared meth and pills he had on hand and ran down the steps. His digging tools were in the boat—he would have to lose those.

He got into the big Wagoneer, turned it around awkwardly in the sand, and moved it out to the track. Leaving the engine running, he quickly twisted a sheet of newspaper, slid several matches around it and tied them off. Then he turned, lit a match to the little homemade fire-maker, and threw it in the door, holding his breath as he ran. Hampered by his injury, he barely reached the car before the trailer blew up, igniting the woods around it, blazing like a giant fireball. As the heat

94

engulfed him, flying sparks hit like tiny missiles, frying his skin and clothes. Frightened by the fire's fury and rising temperatures, he dove into the car, trying to escape from the inferno. He drove like a mad man, scraping the undercarriage again, losing the muffler as he went. Finally, he found the track and gunned the engine. The old car sputtered, then jerked and flew down the sandy road, skittering like a drunken snake with its flattened tire. The track came out near Wakulla Beach, and when the old car hit the pavement, he nearly lost control, but pulled out of the wobbly spin and pushed it for every mile Detroit had made it to run. When he got to HWY 98, he turned right towards Jefferson County, driving blindly, cursing with fear and rage.

Chapter 18

Randall Crum's car radio crackled: "Sheriff, we saw something back there in the Blackwater Swamp, down that side creek, the one with the big trees. It's in territory I don't know real well, maybe close to that smoky peat bog—you know, the volcano. That's real rough terrain back in there, and I couldn't see much. Don't know what it was, but I saw something pink moving down there! I swear I saw it—we ain't got no flamingos up in this neck of the woods, do we? I circled back around a couple of times but I lost it. What do you want me to do?"

"Damnation man, don't you have a brain?" shouted the sheriff, "go back there and look till you figure out what the hell you . . ."

"Whoa, whoa there, what the…?"

Hearing an explosion, Crum said, "You read me? Jeff, talk to me, what is it?" Sheriff Randall Crum paced like a wild dog and nobody spoke to him.

"Golly Jesus," cried the pilot, "there's a fireball coming from down that way. Biggest ball of fire I ever saw, it's even hot up here. I felt the shock of it like an explosion or something. Think I see a blue and white wagon movin' away, but no, black smoke is coverin' everything, Sheriff, it's getting in the motor, gotta clear away…"

CRASH!

The sheriff's team heard the exchange and the sounds of the crash. When it came, dead silence reigned. Then sound erupted as Crum shouted orders; cars squealed, rushing towards the Blackwater Swamp to find their fellow deputies and the pink flamingo they hoped was BJ Hathaway.

* * *

"What have I done to deserve this?" thought Collins. "That bitch has screwed up my life again!"

Suddenly, Jake's moneymakers were gone, his girlfriend and chief supply source was dead, and he was driving a stolen car whose owner might also be dead—which she deserved to be, he thought, in the back.

Driving wild, he pushed the crippled car until it crossed the Jefferson County line, then slowed down and began looking for the dirt road that led to Goose Pasture. He found the one he wanted, and pushing hard against the accelerator, forced it onto the sandy track. Others had been there before him, hardening the track enough to stay in the ruts, but it was still rough driving.

BJ began to stir as she rolled around in the back of the careening car. She was choking, and when she lifted her head searching for air, the car hit a bump, reaming her skull into the tire iron and blessed oblivion once again. Jake thought he heard something but drove on, searching for the road he wanted. He was taking BJ to a sinkhole on the Aucilla River, to a place so isolated and practically impossible to reach that he figured very few people would think of looking there for months to come.

Finding the road he was looking for, he turned left and drove down the logging track, over a metal cattle bridge and into a sabal palm grove. Had he been almost anybody else, the beauty of the morning sun shining through those old trees with the crosshatched stout trunks and shaggy fronds would have brought great pleasure, but he saw none of it in his angst to get rid of both the car and its passenger.

It rained on the Aucilla the night before and raindrops hung like big crystals, glittering on every surface. The jungle, created from huge

97

wild grape vines, thick with age and hundreds of palm trees and palmettos strung together by huge, shimmering spider webs was spectacular. Focused on the potholes and slippery track in his haste to reach the sinkhole, Jake neither saw nor cared for the beauty.

BJ's old car was sturdy under normal conditions, but driving in the densely wooded terrain was rough. To avoid getting stuck, he drove hard over the muddy ruts at an even speed, fighting the old car all the way. Finally, dense shade gave way to light and he saw the clearing he wanted up ahead, just beyond a grove of trees.

Pushing the underbrush and several small trees down in his rush, he nosed the front end of the car to the edge of the sinkhole, trying to get close enough to keep it balanced so he could get out before he tipped it over.

The sides of the big water hole, layered in multiple shades of reddish, gray limestone, dropped straight down to a blue-green pool of bottomless water, its surface partially covered by lush green waterweed.

The front wheels gave as they began to lose purchase on the sand at the sinkhole's edge. Collins put the car in neutral and eased out, leaving the engine running. The sound of a dog baying in the distance sent shivers up and down his spine, reminding him of the throbbing pain in his leg.

Grunting with the effort, he began to push, adrenaline pumping through his veins. Finally, the car slanted at an angle, tipped, and slid down the side of the sinkhole's slippery limestone walls. He jumped back and fell as it took a running dive, wheels spinning wildly in the air, threatening to flip over as it dropped down the side and slid towards the water. Gleefully, he watched it go, laughing as an alligator, frightened out of its den, erupted from the water and skittered up the far side of the steep bank. A line of slider turtles fell off their log as one and a family of mallard ducks flew up, but Jake missed them—he was already pushing off into the woods.

The sudden movement jerked BJ to consciousness. Screaming, she found herself again thrown around like a rag doll. Then she rolled hard into the back door and felt white-hot pain sear through her body at the impact.

Then it stopped. She could hear the wheels spinning; below she heard the gurgle of water.

Blood surged through every pore of her body, giving her superhuman strength and energy in the fight for survival. Desperate to escape, she managed to slip out of the cord Jake had tied her with, and clawed at the roof and sides of the car like a wild animal, but it was hopeless. She was wedged between the spare tire assembly, the seat and the rear door. Coughing, she lay there stunned and hurting, her hands bleeding. She thought she heard laughter from above, and then nothing. All was quiet with the exception of the sound of gurgling water as the car settled, and a dog barking far, far away.

"He's sent me into water," she thought, as the meaning of the sound penetrated the fog in her brain. Again, she renewed the struggle for life, "Oh, my God, I've got to get out—I've got to get out of here!" She screamed when the car jerked, but then it moved no more, nor did she, afraid of setting it in motion again.

Bizarre thoughts ran through her mind, but one made some sense: 'Kick the tail lights out when trapped in the trunk of a car,' said a recent email, but did it mean in a car that might slide further if she moved? She had no way of knowing where she was or how deep the car had sunk.

The old Wagoneer had gone down as Jake planned but then snagged on another partially submerged vehicle, leaving only the rear end barely above the surface. (Stolen cars often found their final resting grounds in North Florida's deep sinkholes, and ironically, this time one of them probably saved BJ Hathaway's life.)

Ignoring the muffled screams of the woman in the car, Jake hobbled back through the palm grove, and then on down to the river, looking for a way out. Frustrated, he searched several cars and trucks on the riverbank, but finally, luck was with him. He hadn't gone far when he found a gray pick-up truck tucked well into the bushes. Sure enough, as he hoped, the keys were in the ignition, just waiting for him.

He was flying down the road when the lone angler emerged from the riverbank and saw what had happened. Jake cackled when he saw the man strike the air with his fists, and kept on driving. The truck was low on gas. Seeing a camouflage hunter's cap and jacket behind the seat, he pulled over, put them on and took the sunglasses from the glove compartment, putting them on, too. He stopped at the only gas station within ten miles of the river, Crawfordville and Perry, J. R. Register's Bait and Tackle, pumped gas and drove off without paying. J.R. looked up just in time to see the color of the pick-up truck—dusty gray, and lifted the phone to call the sheriff's office.

"Yeah, dusty gray, couldn't read the plates but it looked just like Rooster Jones' truck," said Register. "Ain't no way ole' Rooster woulda' stole gas. It wasn't him."

A deputy was dispatched to J.R.'s, but by the time he got there, Jake was in Taylor County. He drove without stopping until he got to Perry. There, he pumped gas again, this time paying for it, used the bathroom, got a coke and a ham sandwich, some beer and a Moon Pie, some peanuts and a newspaper, and took off again, this time headed south on HWY 27, going as far as Hampton Springs. There, he paid cash for room #6 in a run-down motel called the Sundowner, backed into a parking space in the back, stripped off his smoky clothing, crawled into bed and slept like the dead.

Chapter 19

The local First Responders arrived on the scene of the helicopter crash and were already searching for the pilot and his navigator in the dense smoke when the fire trucks screamed in. They crashed through the underlying scrub, but unable to reach the sight of the blast, focused their efforts on keeping the Responders clear of the smoke as they brought the pilot out. They never found the navigator, a new man on the force. The pilot, a ten-year veteran of the Wakulla County Sheriff's Department, had been thrown from the craft in the explosion, landing in a shallow pond nearby. Severely burned and near death, the EMT's rushed him to a clearing in the nearby Southern Magnolia development where a Medical Evacuation helicopter met them and airlifted him down to the burn unit in Gainesville.

The Forest Service sent emergency firefighting helicopters loaded with water and fire suppressants to work the blaze. By the day's end, a late afternoon thunderstorm helped to quench the flames, but the fire settled into the peat bog and simmered on, giving rise yet again to the old rumors of a swamp volcano for years to come. The sheriff staked the burn area to keep out the curious including access from the Blackwater Creek, in hopes of apprehending Jake Collins.

At daybreak the next morning, experts from all over the state converged at the site to seek answers to the blast. For some, it was the first time they had ever set foot in the swamps of North Florida. They found themselves astounded by the complexity of it, and filled with wonder that someone actually lived in the Blackwater Swamp.

The fire had tamped down the undergrowth, making entry to the site less hazardous than it might have been, although embers still burned in some of the trees and the air was acrid.

What they found at the site was sickening: the charred remains of an unidentified body in a melted trash bag inside what was left of the trailer, and remnants of a small blue coupe. They had no way of knowing whose body it was or even if it was female at that point, but by that time, they knew the car was not BJ's.

Sheriff Crum paced back and forth—as he was known to do when deep in thought. "I am pretty sure this is where Jake Collins was holed up," he told his investigative team, "and I'm bettin' he's half-way to Cuba by now, but as to whose body is in that bag, I can't be sure." Then he forgot decorum, his education and everything else in his anger, "Hell ain't hot enough for whoever put that body in that bag and left it to burn, and it better not be BJ Hathaway's. You boys get that stuff up to the state lab in Tallahassee and don't quit until you have something to give me. We got us a mad dog on the loose."

He sent out another APB for BJ's blue and white Wagoneer, this time widening the search area to all of Florida, Georgia, Alabama, and Louisiana. "I'll get that creep if it's the last thing I ever do," he thought to himself.

* * *

There was movement in the underground caverns below. BJ tried not to react, but she knew enough about sinkholes and karst formations to know the danger—the lime rock formations could be shifting due to the explosion back at the trailer.

The car shifted again, and this time water began to seep into the front end, rising slowly. She forced herself to remain calm. The wind picked up during the night as temperatures dropped. The resultant chill seeped into her bones; she felt the old tightness and rattle begin again in her lungs and coughed phlegm up from her toes.

Slowly, she began to feel her way around in the back and managed to sit upright with her head near the rim of the rear door. She

102

could see nothing as it was, but it seemed to her the darkness was getting blacker. Again, she heard the dog baying in the distance and decided the animal was her best bet for survival.

She felt around in the darkness until she found the tire iron. Holding her breath, she gripped it carefully and pulled it from the debris in the back without causing the car to shift again. The car stayed where it was when she pulled it out and she breathed easier for it. She felt for the taillights and when she found one, began hacking to knock it out of its socket, grateful for her natural strength. She had no light and little room to maneuver; her arms were bruised and aching with the asthmatic cough coming out harsh and ragged. It robbed her of some of the strength she needed, but she couldn't quit.

Finally, the light gave way just enough to allow her to grab it and push it through the opening. She tried to call, but the sound came out in a sputter. She cried angry tears of frustration, which made the cough worse, but then she heard the dog bark again, and this time it was nearby.

Foolishly, she whispered, "Here puppy, here puppy," then could have kicked herself. *"How should you call a dog when you are desperate?"* she thought, frantically.

She could hear snuffling as the animal drew nearer. She could barely see it, probably a long legged deerhound, "Good doggie, go get help, you hear me? Go get help." The dog whined and whimpered again and she repeated herself, "Good doggie, go and get help. Help!" The dog paused at the rim of the sinkhole, nosing the ground where the car had been until recently. Then, just as darkness snuffed the last of the light, she saw it move away into the woods.

Carefully, she plugged the light casing back into the hole to keep out the mosquitoes and settled back to rest. Every part of her body hurt and she figured a couple of ribs were broken. "This is like something on TV—it can't be real—it's all a dream," but the pain was real enough, and every breath she drew hurt more than the last.

"If this happened when I was twenty-two instead of fifty-nine, I might have been able to handle it," she thought to herself, "as it is, I wonder if I'll get out of it alive?"

She rummaged around in the back until she found her Red Cross emergency kit, grateful to have put it in there only months before when she moved home to Florida. Fumbling in the darkness, she pulled out the metallic reflective emergency blanket and huddled under it, trying to force the small packets of food open. She ate the contents of one, and managed to get the water packet open and drained that too.

She lay back, thinking about Matt. "Does he know?" she thought sleepily. "I do love that man—why didn't I see it before now?" and began to drift into troubled sleep; she shifted slightly and froze: the car responded to the movement.

Chapter 20

During the night, Jake had nightmares about Robin stuffed into the black plastic trash bag, the yellow trailer and the fire, and the look on BJ Hathaway's face when he tipped the car into the sinkhole. The next morning, when he woke, the bed was soaked with perspiration. When he showered, it was as though the dark, fetid smoke from the explosion still clung to his skin, refusing to come off. He scrubbed until his skin reddened and chafed, but still he felt the heat from the fire and smelled the smoke. He couldn't get away from it and he couldn't go back to sleep, so he went to the pancake house nearby and ordered breakfast, situating himself so he could see the door. While he waited, he read about the explosion in the Hampton Springs Times. BJ Hathaway was listed as a missing person, one man was dead, another was in the burn unit in Gainesville; remnants of an unidentified body were in the morgue at the state lab in Tallahassee undergoing diagnostic testing, and a gray pickup truck, license number FLA### was reported as stolen from the Aucilla River. There was no mention of his name anywhere in the article—not a word. And, there he sat, singed but healthy, cash in his pocket, eating fat pancakes, flirting with the waitress, drinking coffee and reading about it from a distance away.

He smiled to himself, thinking maybe it would work out just fine: maybe he wouldn't have to go all the way south to the Keys or the Everglades after all. He had money and he could start again, buy another trailer or maybe a truck this time, hide out on Live Oak Island, Dark Island or maybe even in Steinhatchee.

Later that morning, he called one of his father's brothers who lived down in Chiefland, told him he'd had a bit of bad luck and asked him if he had any clothes he could spare. His uncle, Jimmy Lee Collins, a fisherman who seldom watched the news and never read the papers, met him at the Suwanee River State Park and gave him some clothes, and $100.00 to boot.

"I don't know what you done this time, boy, but don't ask me, nor none of mine for nothin' more, you hear me?" Jimmy Lee Collins squinted at Jake, then said, "I loved your daddy, boy. He was my baby brother—an' that's the only reason I'm helpin' you. You hear me? Next time you call any of us for help, you won't get it."

Jake took the thin plastic bag and the money. Without another word, Collins clamped down hard on the chew of tobacco in his cheek, climbed back into his pickup and squealed the tires, leaving him standing there holding the clothes and the money.

Later that evening, after a shower, he made his way back to Perry to the notorious '*White's Only*' Club. Having been there in the past, he felt sure of himself in that atmosphere. He sauntered up the steps, rang the hidden buzzer and found welcome at the bar, no questions asked.

Although he was in disguise, he recognized some of the patrons from past visits. He found himself watching three of them carefully—one in particular. They were a bizarre trio that stood out. One of the men, a big man with a wide expanse in the middle, wore brand new overalls and dress shoes, his white hair sleeked back like a televangelist. The second, dressed in a flannel shirt and pressed jeans had perfectly manicured nails, while the third, his long dark hair drawn back in a ponytail, was dressed in jeans and a white dress shirt, the sleeves rolled back to the elbows. The man with the white hair and florid complexion he knew: it was Chesterton Jones, real estate dealer and underground buyer of Indian artifacts. . . the one with the randy son he'd played with down at Wakulla Beach. The watch on his left arm could have fetched the restaurant and everybody in it. The man in the flannel shirt looked familiar to Jake, but he couldn't place him; the other—in the white shirt

106

with the rolled-up sleeves, he'd never seen before. From the conspicuous bulge on his side, Jake figured he was for protection.

Jake smiled to himself, tossed his drink back and after listening to the band for a bit, went back to his room at the motel, whistling. How much would Chessie Jones pay to keep his son's name out of the papers?

Chapter 21

When the explosion shook the ground beneath their feet, Matt and Bobbie Ann knew it had something to do with BJ, but not knowing for sure made the waiting even worse. They spent the night on the covered deck at Bobbie Ann's place, keeping an all-night vigil as helicopters patrolled the skies and sirens rang in the air. Matt paced back and forth on the deck, Chi stalking right behind him, while Bobbie Ann settled in the hammock to wait it out. Restless, she kept thinking about BJ, hoping she still lived, and if she did, that life would be worth living. Finally, she turned the ceiling fan on and lay down, waiting. When a slight breeze came at dawn, it smelled of smoke.

Bobbie Ann was a bit of a mystic, prone to strange dreams and curious happenings, and she felt something calling her to wakefulness. She went to the porch railing and looked out over the river. A fine dusting of ash coated the trees and tinted the air in the soft, waning moonlight. The horizon in the distance was reddened and unnatural; blue lights blinked and the helicopters that had kept them awake the night before now worked the swamp, looking for BJ Hathaway.

The wind was up, blowing in from the Gulf at almost gale force. Shivering, she closed the porch shutters then lay in the hammock again. She tossed for an hour or so then drifted off into semi-sleep, dreaming of fire and sacred ground, Ben, primitive tools and strange music.

Then, as though in a movie theater in 3D vision, she saw BJ in the Wagoneer, down in a sinkhole. The dream was so real that she woke up with a gasp and cried out, "She's in the back of her car. I know it, she's in the back of her car, and it's either near a sinkhole or in one."

The sour taste of acid reflux lingered in her mouth, but she knew it wasn't from the deviled crab she'd had for dinner: she had seen BJ in her dream, seen a grove of ancient palm trees and had felt that old tug she knew as a child: it spoke of death. She had learned to listen to her dreams, and without a second thought, padded into the kitchen to call the sheriff she'd taught when he was just a boy.

Matt roused and started to speak, but she shook her head, pressed auto dial and waited impatiently for the Sheriff's department to answer.

"Hello? This is Bobbie Ann Rice," she said. "I need to speak to Rand— I mean, Sheriff Crum right away. Oh, *he's not there yet*? Yes, yes, thank you—tell him it's about BJ Hathaway. I think I know what has happened to her."

Randall Crum called Bobbie Ann as soon as he got the message. He knew her well enough to know that if she told him something, he could bank on it. After she finished speaking, Randall Crum went into high gear, telling his staff to check the geophysical land maps for all of the sinkholes in Wakulla County and southern Jefferson County then called for back-up from the army reserve unit.

"I gotta have more people on this, sir," he told the commander. "I've got all my units out and now I'm pretty sure that lady is hangin' by a thread—that's if she's still alive."

Chapter 22

Within hours, surface units were checking the ground, moving from sinkhole to sinkhole, hoping to find her. Canine units were most effective in the dense second growth of much of the forest, and it was a dog that took them to BJ. Just off the Aucilla River, Smoke, Deputy Jack Herring's dog, got anxious when he heard baying in the distance and on a hunch, his handler let him follow it. They cris-crossed the Florida Nature Trail numerous times in the search, but finally came on a deerhound, baying at the edge of Clear Sink in some of the roughest ground possible. Coming in from the opposite side of the sinkhole, from Jake's access point they hacked their way through dense vines, downed trees, and rare plant life specimens. An owl hooted as Smoke shot ahead and then disappeared down the side of a big hole in the ground. He skidded to a halt near a partially submerged blue and white battered Wagoneer. By that time, just the top of the back and the rear wheels were visible, as it had continued to slip further into the cold water, inch by inch.

Inside, BJ, exhausted and cold from hypothermia heard the commotion. She had almost given up on the deerhound—the dog barked, ran away for a while, and then returned to stay nearby, howling occasionally, and finally she found comfort in her presence. When she heard trucks, dogs barking and what sounded like a dog sliding down towards her, she tried to lift her head, but was unable to move very far. Multiple cuts, bruises, stiffened muscles and fear of unsettling the car, refused to allow her much movement; instead, she began to cough, which excited Smoke. He tried to run back up the steep side of the sinkhole but slid back down, dislodging the car even more. Deputy Herring, seeing what was going to happen, called the dog, "Halt, Boy. Halt!" and the dog skidded to a stop just before he collided with the car again. He heard the woman coughing and began to whine, looking down at her and then back up to his handler. The deerhound kept up her howling, now running around the edge of the big sinkhole in excitement.

"You're okay, Girl, it's okay" said Herring. "You'll be alright. You've done real good. Stay!" but the deerhound continued to bounce around on the lip of the sinkhole, refusing to leave, her loud bay constant in the background. "Look what I did," said that bark, "look what I did!"

Herring called his position in and waited for backup. There was no way to get down there without making the situation worse, so he called out to her, "Ms. Hathaway? BJ, are you down there? Can you answer me?"

He waited, hoping to hear something, but between the two dogs, her answers were lost. Finally, he saw the tail light move, and when it fell out, he yelled, "Hang on ma'am, we've got help comin'. Stay calm. We'll get you out just as soon as we can, okay?"

BJ heard him, but she was too tired to respond. Just pushing the tail light out again was more effort than she had the extra energy to expend. She lay there, huddled under the Red Cross blanket, her head pushed up against the tail light opening, trying to stay calm and trying to keep breathing. She was so cold. Just as she closed her eyes, Smoke's black Belgian nose pushed through the opening and he licked her face. It was warm—the powerful touch of one animal to another, and it was life giving. She had never particularly liked big dogs—other than Chi, but this big dog's licks were welcome. She could hear the deerhound baying again, and lifting her head, swore to herself that if the dog who kept her company all night needed a home, it had one for life. Then she apologized to her Maker for any disparaging remarks she might have made about dogs in the past. Her sense of humor kicked in when she realized how idiotic her thinking was and began to laugh, but the sound

111

turned to harsh coughing that wouldn't stop and hurt her ribcage, bringing angry tears to her eyes.

The deputy, standing on the sinkhole's rim heard the coughing and called, "Emergency, I don't care what you do, somebody get the medics in here. This lady is really sick."

* * *

Jake ate a quick breakfast at the Pancake House and decided he'd been in one place too long. Leaving the parking lot, he walked over to the motel, got his stuff and cleared out. After wiping away his fingerprints, he left the truck where it sat. Hitching a ride to Dark Island on a hunch, he arrived just before noon. True to his nature, he nosed around until he found an easily accessed unoccupied cabin, broke in and made himself at home. Dark Island was an isolated half-moon of beach with well-built vacation homes seldom occupied by management from the nearby paper mill, and it suited his purposes quite well. He figured he could forage in Steinhatchee, and be a lone fisherman without stirring up too much interest, at least until he heard what had happened to BJ at the sinkhole. For some reason, he couldn't leave—not yet, anyway. The whole thing in the Blackwater Swamp drew him like a magnet. It had been too easy to escape, but he wasn't complaining. The silence about his part in the explosion, however, made him nervous and more than a little curious.

The more he thought about it, the more he believed it was just possible that he could return to the Indian burial grounds at Magnolia without being detected. If he found what he thought was in there, he'd be stinking rich and could live like a king on one of the Keys down in South Florida, or maybe the Bahamas, maybe buy an island of his own, he thought, giggling at his own humor.

Chapter 23

As soon as the car was located, Sheriff Crum put a call through to Bobbie Ann. She was standing in a window watching the smoke, when the call came through.

"You were right again, Bobbie Ann" he said. "She was in Ben's old Wagoneer in a sinkhole—just exactly like what you saw in your dream down to the last detail. By the way, did you see a dog in that dream? No? Well, I'll tell you more about it later. We've got work to do down here. Y'all stay where you are, I'll send somebody for you when we get her out. If you have any more dreams, keep me posted, 'cause I'm listenin'."

* * *

Deputy Herring was relieved to hear the sound of choppers overhead. The deerhound fled into the woods as trees waved wildly in the wind. Finally, the emergency unit's big crash truck came through the undergrowth, this one following roughly the same track Jake's mad drive made, but with far more power. Within minutes of arrival, the Wakulla County Sheriff's Department dive team donned their wetsuits and assessed the situation. What they saw almost made them give up hope at first, but down they went, sliding on damp limestone walls with few footholds.

Kate Treadway, a diver with fourteen years in law enforcement, spoke to BJ as they worked, "Eh, Ms. Hathaway, it's me, Kate

Treadway—remember me from the Green Guides course? I sat next to you all the way through. Anyway, we're going to get you out of here. It's likely to be real rough, but since you've made it this far, I think you can do it. You won't be alone—I'll try to stay as close as I can. Can you hear me BJ? Say something, please!"

The officer, worried that BJ had lost consciousness, was relieved to hear scratching, but the wracking cough that followed got her attention. She continued to talk, saying anything that came to her mind as they worked.

The slick limestone sides of the sinkhole made finding purchase to secure the wrecked car difficult. The team worked quickly as the sheriff directed from the rim and by late afternoon, they were able to attach the rear axle of the car to heavy chains. The wind whipped palm trees around like mop heads gone crazy, and a sense of urgency was in the air as temperatures began to drop in the already cool sinkhole. Deputy Treadway signaled to the men in the tow truck to start backing up. The car shuddered and fell loose from its mooring on the submerged vehicle on which it had rested, hovering directly over the big hole, nose down. The movement sloshed water up around BJ's head. Panicked, she held on to the edge of the light socket to keep from sliding down, screaming with pain.

Kate Treadway looked up at one of her co-workers as they worked, anguish in her face, but she continued to speak in careful, measured tones to the woman trapped in the car as though it was something they did every day. She nodded and they began to retrieve the vehicle inch by inch. The deerhound was back but this time it was quiet, and watchful. The Belgian, who had made its way to the top, stood watching next to the hound as the battered vehicle moved up the side of the sinkhole, then onto solid ground, and gently rolled to its rightful position.

They found BJ, crumpled, broken, wet and barely recognizable, but alive. Jubilant, the deerhound tried hard to climb in after her. The medics took control of the situation, gently lifting the woman, still dressed in her sodden, dirty nightgown and the torn pink chenille robe

114

out of the car that was nearly her coffin. She lay on the stretcher in shock, barely breathing; the rattle in her chest the only sound she made as the medics administered first aid and covered her with layers of warmed blankets. The coughing continued, making every breath difficult, but as she warmed, she tried to speak in spite of it.

"That dog—the hound, where is it? That dog's been here with me all night," she said as Deputy Herring came up with the long-legged black and tan dog on a leash. BJ smiled when it tried to jump up on the stretcher. "You want a home, girl?" she wheezed, fighting for every ragged breath. "You've got one...with me if you need it." Then with her hand on the smooth head of the dog, her own head dropped back onto the pillow, her eyes rolled back and the medics went to work to resuscitate her.

Relief flooded through her friends when they got the news of BJ's rescue. Bobbie Ann flew down the steps, forgetting caution, to tell Matt.

"They've found her Matt!" The two friends hugged and danced around the patio until the sheriff's car drove up and the back door opened. "Sheriff Crum asked me to give you folks a ride to the hospital," said the young deputy. "Can you come now?"

Joy, shock, and grief were close companions as the friends raced to the hospital in Tallahassee at breakneck speed with the blue lights whirling overhead. They spoke little, Bobbie Ann, remembering the portent of her dream, now fearing the potential for death.

BJ, normally a robust, strong woman was asleep when they arrived in her room. She vaguely resembled the BJ Hathaway they knew: the strong face was pale and looked fragile, with black circles under her closed eyes, her face and arms cut, bruised and puffy, one arm in a sling, her ribs bandaged, and oxygen hose in her nose. The unruly black and white hair fanned out over the pillow like a tattered halo. That she was alive was a miracle, but whether she would survive to recovery was the question. They all knew it as they listened to her struggle for breath, each one when it came out, a deadly rattle.

115

Bobbie Ann and Matt huddled together nearby, listening as BJ struggled to breathe, afraid to take their eyes off her. Initial joy at her rescue segued into fear when they first saw her, then fear turned to anger, followed by rage, bonding them into a cohesive force. They were resourceful people with a mission now—they would help find Jake Collins whether Sheriff Randall Crum welcomed their help or not. Matt fingered the gun in his pocket. There were no guarantees of what would happen when *he* next saw Jake Collins.

Chapter 24

Meanwhile, the deerhound was eating better than it had for some time. In fact, the dog was enjoying royal status as the key instrument in finding BJ Hathaway. Little did anyone know that it might also be key in catching BJ's kidnapper as well.

Deputy Herring put the hound in the kennel next to Smoke and ran a check from the scratched tag on the torn leather collar. It turned out it had been given up for lost during hunting season. If the exposed ribs meant anything at all, the dog had been living a subsistence life in the woods ever since. The owner, Ray Crosby, when he heard of the dog's recovery and the work it had done to discover BJ Hathaway, told how he had spent days roaming the woods on the Aucilla trying to find the dog, and had finally given up. After hearing about Coon's heroic deeds that day, he was tempted to pick the dog up and take it back to the house down in Cody, but BJ's story and her offer of a new home changed all of that. Crosby gave up all rights to the dog and signed it over to the sheriff's department.

The next day, the Wakulla Times ran Coon's photograph next to BJ's in the report of the day's events. BJ, regaining consciousness, saw it on local television later that day and tried to laugh at the dog's comic expression, but the pain was so intense tears fell instead. "Y'all do know that I promised that dog a home, don't you?"

Her friends, happy to see signs of life, gathered round and laughed for her. Matt told her, "BJ, Randall has Coon down at the station keeping Deputy Herring's dog Smoke, company. During the search, Sgt. Smoke heard Coon howling and found her on the edge of the sinkhole where you were found trapped. That dog is definitely a hero. The owner, Ray Crosby, already signed it over to the sheriff's department. They'll take good care of it, you know that."

BJ coughed, and then, her humor returning, said, "Well, I will have to speak with Randall about that. I've promised that hound dog a home, and I intend to make it happen. We'll have to give Smoke and his handler a reward. That should make the good Sheriff happy enough to do what I want him to do." Then, in a most uncharacteristic, genteel southern accent, she turned to Matt and said, "Matt Walker, I will not have a dog named 'Coon.' So help me that dog will have a new name by the time she comes to live with us."

She never knew what she had said, nor did she see the expression on Matt Walker's face when she said it. His surprise was real—had something changed since the ordeal with Jake? He knew enough about shock to put little stock in it, but somehow, his heart had lifted considerably when he left her side later that night. In all their time together, living in the same house had never come up.

* * *

Knowing BJ was lucky to be alive, Matt and Bobbie Ann finally left her to the nurses and walked down to the cafeteria to get a bite to eat. They weren't really hungry, but it seemed to be the right thing to do when a loved one was in the hospital.

Matt got a big salad and a hotdog, Bobbie Ann some yogurt. They took their repast to a small table in the far corner so they could watch for the Sheriff if he came in; neither wanted to talk.

She said nothing as he devoured the hotdog before touching the salad. "What are you looking at me like that for? This is my version of comfort food, so leave me alone, woman!"

Smiling, she got up, went back into the cafeteria and came out with one for herself. She ate it slowly and found that, strangely enough, the simple hotdog was comforting, but then so was the yogurt. When she finished, she sat back and closed her eyes for a moment.

They were sitting in a drowsy, companionable silence, drinking coffee when Randall Crum came striding in, all business in his uniform, accompanied by one of his deputies.

"I just left BJ, y'all," he said. "She's gone into pneumonia and the asthma has kicked up big-time, but I believe she's gonna make it."

They were laughing and congratulating one another when he broke in, "But I've got more news, and it's serious. We've got an ID from the DNA in a hair in the little blue car and in that melted garbage bag from the trailer: it's Robin England all right. Her friend Lilly, who works at the Riverside, called her in missin' early this mornin'. Turns out the girl's was seein' Collins, and she's the one who's been "shopping," for him. She's been in trouble off and on—mostly for drugs, but nothing as bad as this. Now, she's lost her life." He sat down and shook his head. "I just don't understand how stuff like this happens, I don't care how many times I see it. I may just retire after this. Go fishin.' Don't think I can take much more."

Bobbie Ann touched his arm gently, saying, "Randall, look at me." He finally looked up and saw in her eyes the respect he needed and was comforted. He put his hand over hers for a moment, patted it, and then went on, "We think Jake's holed up somewhere in Taylor County, because he stole a truck from a fisherman on the Aucilla. I've got an APB out, but he's been lying' pretty low. Ain't nobody seen hide nor hair of anybody looks like him here or there bout's, but there's been some artifacts pawned over that direction this afternoon that had to have come from here."

He turned to Bobbie Ann, "I understand you realized somethin' was missin' from the river house. I need you to come down to the office later this afternoon and see what we've got, okay?" Bobbie Ann looked down at her hands and then back up to him, tears in her eyes and answered, "You know I will, Randall. I'll do whatever I have to do to get that man behind bars again."

Crum nodded and added, "You bet! What I do know is that if he's still alive, and I'm bettin' he is, he'll be back. I've got deputies watchin' BJ round the clock. She don't need to be alone until we catch him. None of you do—you understand what I'm sayin'? All three of you were close to Ben and all three of you are potential targets, not just BJ."

Chapter 25

Bobbie Ann stayed with BJ that night, and while it was difficult to leave, Matt knew Chi had to be let out soon, and he wanted to check their properties while it was still light. Before going down to the river, he drove into Crawfordville and stopped by the canine unit to meet the dog named Coon.

He knew Smoke already and greeted the Belgian with his handler by his side, but it was to the deerhound his attention was drawn. Cautious at first, Coon warmed up quickly after a treat and a rub, and Matt promised to come by for her when BJ was well enough.

* * *

Chi greeted him with an eagerness that went beyond feeling neglected for a couple of days. He knew there was trouble, and he could smell the scent of another dog on Matt's hands and pants legs. He pranced and sniffed until Matt finally pushed him out of the door to do his business. After running around the property several times, and stopping more than once, he ran back up the stairs, nosed the screened-door open, and tried to get into Matt's lap as he sat on the porch facing the water.

"Hey, what's up, Old Boy? You know you are too big to be a lap dog!" Chi, however, was determined to make a nest for himself in Walker's lap. It was obvious from the beginning that it wasn't going to work, but still the dog was determined to get comfortable. Finally, Matt hugged him and got up, spilling the red dog onto the decking. He went into the kitchen and fished around until he found a new dog bone. He pitched it to him and went back to his chair, the soft leather squeaking gently as he settled back into the seat. Chi, satisfied at last, dropped down at the man's feet and lay over them, gnawing at the bone, but keeping one eye cocked in the direction of his best friend.

Restless, Matt couldn't keep his eyes off of the soft red fire dancing in the distance. He was plenty worried about BJ and the two big questions that loomed over all: what was Jake Collins' location, and would BJ ever feel safe on the river again.

Chapter 26

Jake stared out over the dark water. He was getting lonely in the complete absence of human companionship. Every day he listened for news about BJ, but word of her was hard to get. He knew she survived the sinkhole, having seen the rescue on television at the café, but now he worried about the damned sheriff, Randall Crum. There had been bad blood between the two men for years and Jake figured his life was forfeit if Crum got a hold of him again. He grinned to himself, thinking he'd just have to get to the god-almighty sheriff first, because he had business to take care of with BJ Hathaway.

He lit a cigarette, poking the lighted match into a crab hole in the soft white sand. A translucent little sand crab shot out in panic, steaming. Jake cackled with what passed for humor with him, flung his cigarette into the darkness and went back to the cabin where he drank a quart jug of cheap beer and sank into a drunken sleep.

* * *

BJ spent several weeks in the hospital recovering from her wounds, and undergoing breathing therapy for her lungs. At her release, Bobbie Ann and Matt wrangled over where she would go to complete her recuperation. Sheriff Crum stepped in to settle the matter of where BJ would stay.

"Listen, you two, she needs both of you dunce heads. Matt, I want you to take her to your place and keep Chi near her at all times, and that hound dog, too if you're ready to deal with it. Never leave her alone. Bobbie Ann, if he has to leave, I want you there with her. I will keep a deputy in the neighborhood, camera surveillance on the place and wiretap it, too, with your permission. We know its Jake Collins, and from experience with him in the past, we know he *will* come back to finish this business. Let's just hope his low profile in the press has worked. We've got a decoy over at her place, too, so we've got you covered," said the big man with a smile that only partially hid his concern.

Bobbie Ann and Matt brought their patient home by ambulance in style, with the EMT's taking her up the steps and settling her into Matt's easy chair to rest.

Later in the afternoon, Matt and BJ watched the sun sink behind the trees, speaking little but thinking deep. They spoke even less during the evening. He cooked an omelet, fried bacon and toast, which they ate in companionable silence. When it was time for sleep, there were no thoughts of romance involved for either of them. Both were dazed by the events of the last few weeks and needed to sit back to let them digest. Neither wished to be alone; both were grateful for the company.

BJ had been in Matt's house plenty of times, but tonight was different. She was tired, her defenses were down and something in their relationship dynamic had changed since the incident with Jake Collins. While she was just a year older than Matt, she thought men aged better than women did and suddenly, it made her feel insecure. He was still good looking and very appealing in a rugged way—surely there were younger women dangling their wares in front of him … how could she expect him to pay serious attention to her, especially since she'd been through hell after Jake's attack and still felt and looked it. That thought strengthened her resolve; she did not want to embarrass herself. Not with this man, whose friendship she valued above all things, so she steeled herself, forcing restraint in her response to him.

They wrangled over who would take the bed, but finally Matt won BJ over. "Listen, you mule-headed woman, you are my guest and you nearly died just a few weeks ago. I would appreciate it if you'd shut up, go in there, get your shower and go to bed. I am too tired to argue with you. I'm going to sleep on the sofa and that's the end of it. You hear me?"

Chi watched them spar, a puzzled look on his grizzled face. Looking from one to the other, he wagged his tail slowly, as though trying to figure out who was going to win.

BJ, keeping her face expressionless during the tirade, watched Matt closely, wanting to run her fingers through his hair, longing to feel the roughness of his skin next to hers. She wanted the comfort of his arms around her, needed to press her chest closely to his to feel his heart beat. She knew he would come to her if she asked, but now that she had erected the barrier to intimacy with him in her mind, she couldn't back away from it.

Sensing BJ's mind at work, Matt turned away to get fresh sheets. She listened to his voice as he talked to the dog. It reminded her of the sound of crackling fire on new wood, and she felt warmed by it. She accepted Matt's offer of the bed, but slept light, aware of every breath he took in the next room. When the painkillers finally kicked in, she relaxed, inhaling the scent of him on the pillow. She was too tired to let her mind play with it for long and soon fell into deep, dream-filled sleep.

That night, BJ dreamed about the river, but it was in the form of a nightmare at first. She had dreams as a child, but as an adult, they became knowing dreams and often took her to places of the mind and spirit she couldn't go in waking hours.

She was a child again, floating on the surface of black, Blackwater. The day was warm but the water was cold. Tall trees hid the sun, casting dark shadows over the black, Blackwater. Blackwater below, blue sky above; enormous trees on all sides, embracing one another above, tops flattened against the sky in an effort to grow even higher above, tops flattened against the sky in an effort to grow even higher above earth's surface to reach the sun. Thick, swirling pollen clung in places to the surface, writing notes to the observer. Even shadows looked alive and full of promise.

'Shall I put my hand in,' she asked herself. 'I feel compelled to touch it.' She allowed her hand to be drawn into the darkness below, sucked into an opaque darkness that obliterated the light.

What followed changed the child forever, imprinting her with a powerful knowledge that went far beyond what her unformed mind could understand.

As from a great distance the child she once was, looked into the dark water, and saw her own face, a round, white orb with great, curious eyes staring back.

"Come," said the Blackwater, "Come, let me take you. Let me envelope you. Become one with me and your spirit will be joined to the life within me which never dies."

Her child-spirit responded as one who recognizes ancient wisdom and she embraced the appeal of the voice in her mind. Suddenly, she felt herself drawn back and down into the water, but the message became one of pain. She struggled but could not escape, feeling anguish, fear and deepest dread as the silken depths enveloped her body, mind and soul.

"Why," she called out, "Why Blackwater? You called me and told me you would fill me with life—this is death. I am afraid; it hurts."

It was then the Blackwater's voice spoke to her soul saying, "Now, you will begin to understand. You, who came from my depths, and to whom I gave life, are a part of my destruction. You must experience my pain and know my loss. I have chosen you. I have called you here to stop the destruction because we are all inter-joined and interconnected.

The child that she was cried out, "Black, Blackwater, what must I do? How can I live again? Your blackness has invaded my soul. I cannot live, your blackness is my death."

"No!" roared the water in a voice that shot through her entire body, "You will live with my darkness of spirit because I am life! You will speak my truth and bring its light back to the earth once again."

BJ woke from the dream soaked in perspiration, limp hair clinging to her face. Martha kneaded her chest, a worried expression on her beautiful black and white face.

Hearing BJ cry out, Matt and Chi raced into the room to check on their patient. Martha arched her back at first, her eyes glassy with fright, and then backed down. If Matt noticed the tear-stained pillow, he said nothing and neither did BJ. He guided her into the bathroom, changed the damp sheets and helped her stagger back to bed without asking questions.

Matt had difficulty drifting off again, knowing BJ was in his bedroom, wanting to give comfort, but nothing in her expression had given him an invitation to do so. He had held her earlier, helping her get up from the easy chair, and the closeness stirred feelings for her that wanted to find expression again, but no way was he going to take a chance on driving her away now. She had been through hell, and needed space. He could give her that. He thought there might be a possibility for more, if he treaded lightly and gave her time.

BJ was a beautiful woman in her own way, he mused, and very much an individual, but nothing about her was simple. Even in her late-fifties, she was attractive in a long-legged, high-waisted way—sort of like a mustang that had long run wild in the desert. A strong face, framed by crazy, streaked black and white hair, and high cheekbones that flanked the long, straight nose culminated in soft, full lips over strong white teeth, always ready to curve into an easy laugh or spontaneous argument. Everything about her fascinated him. She was interesting and

127

compelling, and he wanted nothing more than to spend as much time with her as he could. Knowing she slept in his bed was deeply arousing, giving him no rest. Hearing her toss and turn, and on occasion cry out, he wanted to comfort her, but stayed where he was. She was in charge, and he could wait.

The next morning, he got up at dawn, made a pot of coffee and called Chi for their walk. Together, they went down to the river to check on the eagle's nest. BJ heard them leave and limped out to the porch to watch the man and his dog in their habitat. She longed to be with them, but she was so tired—more tired than she remembered in all her life. Too tired to talk, walk or even think, but there was much to be done. She needed to call the board of directors together and get the restoration project at Goose Pasture jump-started again. It seemed only right to begin work on the area where she faced the specter of death, but the thought of it made her head ache.

She stayed on the deck watching the man and his dog for a while, and then made her way back to the living room. A cup of hot, black coffee did much to alleviate her stress, but feeling the pain of her injuries she went back to bed and was asleep when Matt and Chi came back from their walk.

They settled into a companionable routine for the next few weeks, until Coon's arrival, which set the temporary household on its ear. An outside dog, she needed to be house trained, and taught not to bark at everything that moved. Trying to find her place in the family, she horned in on Chi's favorite spot near Matt and nearly lost her life over it, then settled in near BJ and Martha. Surprisingly, Martha accepted the dog without a fight, sensing an ally. BJ and Matt bandied about the notion of changing Coon's name, until BJ settled on Sasha, named for a dog she knew as a girl.

Chapter 27

At the cabin, Jake settled in. He closed the flimsy drapes, and using duct tape, sealed the windows with oversized trash bags he got at the dollar store. He craved isolation now, and folks would get suspicious if they saw light in the cabin. With no electricity, he needed to find some way to stay warm, but he was afraid to light a fire in the fireplace. That time of year few big city owners braved the chill winds coming off the marshes, but a local fisherman might see the light and get suspicious. He found a battery lantern in the cupboard, blankets in the bedroom closet, flannel shirts and a quilted down jacket and began to make himself at home.

The next morning, he walked into Steinhatchee, picked up a newspaper, and made his way down to Roy's. He was just in time to hear the Cable 13 reporter say that BJ Hathaway was still alive. He saw them pulling the battered blue and white Jeep Wagoneer up from the sinkhole and then saw the long-legged hound. Silently, he cursed—it was the same dog that been there barking when he pushed the car over the edge. Hiding his anger behind the coffee cup, he stopped eating when he heard about the dog leading the rescue team to the woman in the sinkhole not far from the Florida Nature Trail. He had forgotten the trail ran through there.

Muttering under his breath, he said, "I should've killed that damned dog when I had the chance." Rubbing the festering wound on the back of his thigh, he vowed that both the deerhound and the red chow mix were dead dogs if he ever got close enough to kill them. And he would. Jake never forgot a wrong—that dog had wronged him just like the dog that bit him, and now, thanks to a damned dog, that nosy bitch was alive. It just didn't seem possible she could have survived that fall and being in a partially submerged car all night, but she had, and now he was going to have to go back and finish what he had begun. There could be no more loose ends. She had to go, and so did the damned dog.

Both the griddle cook and the waiter serving Jake saw his face when he heard the news, which blared all over the restaurant. They noticed that he seemed to pay special attention to the sinkhole rescue story, and then saw him quickly thumb through the paper as though looking for something.

They assumed he was renting somewhere on the coast nearby, which was not unusual. He ordered the same thing every day: three fried eggs, hash-browns extra crisp, fried steak and black coffee. He refused to make small talk, and he never left a tip after the first visit. Many visiting fishermen ate at the restaurant, but most were friendly, and nearly all of them tipped well. As a result, the staff gave him what he ordered, and nothing more, but they also watched him carefully. There was something about him that didn't seem right. Besides, he never looked any of them in the eye and kept his cap down low, tight curls fighting confinement at his neck. As a result, they knew more about him than he could have imagined...

Angry, he left Roy's, his breakfast half-eaten. The newspaper, folded to the story about Betsy Jane Hathaway's rescue, still lay on the table. Tamara, his server, took the paper and stuffed it under the counter with her purse in case something should come of it. Something about that man bothered her, and she'd be ready if anybody came in asking questions.

Jake stopped by the dollar store again, and bought some long-johns then went to the bait and tackle store and bought beer, chips and bait, and made his way back to the cabin virtually unnoticed. The shallow beach near the marshes was completely deserted, just the way he liked it. Relaxed about as much as strung wire, he moved at a steady gait, without haste, sure now of his disguise but always watchful.

130

Once inside, he dropped all pretenses and raved until the venom was spewed out. Spent and exhausted, he looked for the newspaper, realized he'd left it behind and drank cheap beer from a quart bottle until oblivion overtook him. Sometime during the day he woke, smoked a cigarette and drank more beer, then sank into a deep sleep that lasted until morning. When he woke, it was with renewed determination. He'd stay under cover for a while until things simmered down on the river, then go back for BJ Hathaway.

There could be no loose ends!

Chapter 28

Collins stayed on Dark Island through the winter months, keeping a low profile. The owners of the cabin failed to show when the weather warmed, so he stayed on. Most of the locals knew the stranger was living somewhere on the island. He brought so little attention to himself that even they didn't know where, and certainly didn't care as long as he made no trouble.

He let his hair grow longer, tying it back in a ponytail, cultivated a thick, full beard, wore a hunting cap most of the time, and bought some cheap reading glasses to wear in public. He'd sold some of the meth he brought with him at the club in Perry, but was staying low to avoid detection. He was bored. He dared not try to set up a cook operation, even with the new shake and bake method. Something told him the Taylor County sheriff would offer no mercy if he was caught. He couldn't communicate with any of his old contacts, so Jake became even more of a loner than ever. He avoided even the company of the friendly waitress with the inviting black eyes and big rump at the diner in Hampton Springs, using his own hand to relieve his sexual needs.

Taking up fishing as a cover, he smudged the tags on the boat docked near the cabin and set out to look for sites to dig. At first, the pickings were slim. He didn't know the area, but he knew the signs, and knew his way around the woods even better. Old Ben had taught him well.

One afternoon in the early fall, he hit pay dirt near Steinhatchee. He'd been watching an abandoned trailer built high on stilts for some time. He observed the Spanish bayonets and century plants hugging the pilings, downed limbs, unkempt yard, and uncut grass. There were no fresh tracks in the grass—the place was deserted and suited to his needs.

One day, staying close to shore, he made his way through a sudden hard rain, docked and ran through wild honeysuckle and stinging nettle, seeking cover. He was making his way up the steps when he saw the cypress-log cabin almost hidden in the jungle behind it.

Finding little of value in the trailer, he worked his way to the cabin through dense undergrowth in what was now a drizzle, and was about to step in when he heard a conspicuous rattle near his right foot. Freezing at the sound, he backed out slowly, but not before seeing dozens of rattlers writhing in a mating dance inside the husk of deteriorating logs. Still, the rattler struck, long, venomous fangs snagging in the thick, white, rubber, fishing boots he wore.

Shaking, he beat the snake off with a heavy limb and left the reptiles to their ritual, giving the cabin wide berth. He was about to go back to the trailer when he saw the telltale rise among the palmetto fans in the distance.

His senses tingled with excitement. "If that's what I think it is," he thought, "I may be home free."

Taking the stick he still carried, he made his way to what appeared to be a midden and prodded the edges, then the middle until he found pottery shards. He broke some of them, the snake encounter making him more careless than usual.

"Miccosukee," he thought, running his fingers across the familiar design. Grinning, he said to himself, "Ben Taylor, your training is about to pay off— just not the way you planned, old man."

Chuckling, he circled the ancient mound of sand and oyster shells. When he saw the lip of a pot he pushed the sand away with his bare hands and brought up a perfect specimen. Putting it under his shirt, he snapped his jacket to hold it safe and made his way past the orgasmic frenzy in the cabin. The sun was setting, but there was enough light to see a sleek boat and two men in gray coast guard uniforms looking at his boat.

"Looks like old man Pickles' boat to me," said one, "but he's over at the nursin' home in Medart, if he's still livin', that is."

"We'll I'm pretty sure it shouldn't be here, and we ain't gonna leave it, no matter who's usin' it," said the other man. "There's another storm brewing behind this one. You tie it behind our boat, and let's head on back to Shell Point before it hits. We'll come back first thing in the mornin' and see if there's anything going on."

Cursing, Jake watched from the stand of trees until they took the boat and left, then he stomped up the steps to the trailer to forage, knowing it was too late to try and hike back to the cabin on Dark Island.

"It's time for me to head out of here," he said to himself, "but I ain't leavin' without the treasure that's hid in that mound over there. It's finders/keepers."

The trailer was stuffy as the storm approached over the Gulf of Mexico, and he opened the windows to let in the breeze and clear the air. There was just enough light to see black ants an inch long running up and down the walls, and when he went back to the bedroom, he found massive spider webs. Discouraged from sleeping back there, he 'made do' with the rusted daybed in the front room.

After the storm subsided and the night air cooled, it was under shabby quilts near the bay windows that he slept. A full moon lit the room as the storm clouds dissipated, and a slight breeze rustled the sabal palm fronds near the windows, but Jake noticed none of it in his need for sleep.

He was up with the sun, and ignoring the blackbirds cackling in the palms, made his way back to the midden, digging with his stick in sand heavy and damp from the storm. He had no time for niceties and dug with haste, again breaking things in his angst, but not before pulling

134

out more pots, ornaments including a heavy gold ring, possibly Spanish, and gold coins. Stuffing it all into pillowcases stolen from the trailer, he left the burial mound desecrated in his wake, and set out to get the pot he'd left in the trailer the night before.

Chapter 29

The coast guard officers, who went to Marty Pickle's cabin the next morning, saw the house had been lived in for some time, the windows sealed shut with black bags and duct tape, and knew they were onto something serious.

"Whoever's been livin' here didn't want nobody to know about it," said the deputy. "Hey, Keith, come look at this," and there, by the bed were yellowing stacks of Leon, Jefferson and Wakulla County newspapers, all carefully folded to articles about the BJ Hathaway kidnapping case, and the explosion off Blackwater Creek from the previous summer.

"Keith get me some back up and bring the fingerprint kit," he said. "Then you get Amos and Trousdale and tell'em go to that trailer where we found Pickles' boat. We may get our man if we move fast enough. I'm bettin' it's the same one we saw yesterday, and he's just moved his operation over there. Get somebody to check around the restaurants and groceries and bars, too. I think we got us a killer on the loose."

By noon, servers at Roy's spilled everything they had observed about the man with the curly sandy hair and ragged beard, getting an earful about the non-tipping fisherman who came in almost every day. They heard about his inordinate interest in anything pertaining to the Blackwater Swamp explosion and BJ Hathaway. Nobody knew his name, where he was staying or who he was. One of the servers remembered, however, an incident with three oddly dressed strangers and the man's quick departure. When she pulled the yellowing newspaper from under the counter, the deputy was in touch with the sheriff before he hit the door.

* * *

Jake was getting ready to leave when he heard the Coast Guard boat. Hidden by ragged draperies in the morning's half-light, he watched the men as they stealthily made their way to his hideaway, guns drawn. He took a chair, waited at the door, and when it opened, slammed the deputy over the head, knocking him to the ground below, pushing the other one down the steps. Jumping over the man in his haste, he raced to their boat, feeling the old injury in his leg quiver as he ran. Jumping in, he dumped his treasure on the seat beside him without ceremony, flipped the ignition switch and flew out over the water, leaving a huge wake and two angry officers behind.

He laughed when he heard them calling for help on the radio, but it was too late: they weren't fast enough to catch him. Jake was wily; he knew they'd be hot on his trail, but he was almost to the Gulf and open water by the time their backup arrived.

Even after a year, his bad leg throbbed from exertion, but there was no time to stop and check it for damage. Leaving the boat in a cove, he hitchhiked down to the Econfina River Lodge camping ground, took off his hat, put on the glasses and borrowed a phone at the lodge office. He had a little business to wrap up with Ms. Hathaway and Matt Walker before heading south to the Everglades, but it was time to call his chips in from Mr. Chesterton Jones before he did.

Chapter 30

"Hey, Chess, it's me, Jake Collins," he said when the man picked up the phone. "I got some stuff I want to move real quick—good quality. You interested?"

"Where the hell are you, and what are you calling *me* for Collins?" said Jones. "Anything you've got has blood stains on it, now. You'd better stay as far away from here as you can get, man. It's been a year since you almost killed BJ Hathaway, but the law is still on full alert looking for you—they're just keeping quiet about it."

Something in his voice made Jake smile—he was still famous, still a threat! He was also holding a winning card in his hands: Chesterton Jones with his lust for collectible artifacts, and a list of illegal transactions a yard long that he, Jake Collins knew about personally.

"I ain't particularly worried about it, Chessie. Besides, I seen *you* a couple of times lately with some mighty suspicious characters," he said. "Seein' the company you been keepin' I'd say you been up to no good. The right word dropped in the right place could get you in a peck a'trouble. Well, let's get down to business—I ain't got much time: I got some prime stuff that'll make your head spin when you see it. Miccosoukee, yeah! It can be yours for a mere $20,000 cash."

Jones ignored the comments about his recent activities—he was all attention at the mention of Miccosoukee artifacts, forgetting caution in his greed. "I am interested, but I must see the items before committing, Collins. You know that," he said.

Jake grinned into the receiver. "I'm at the Econfina Lodge & Camp Ground off HWY 98. Be here just after sundown, alone, or I will find that sex-starved boy of yours and cut his balls off. You understand me?"

Jones blubbered a moment before answering, "What do you know about my son? He's never done anything to you and neither have I. You sure seemed to like the money we've paid you over the years."

"That boy hit on my woman after we got together," said Jake. "Bought drugs from her and then tried to rape her. You didn't know about that, did you? It wouldn't be too hard to get an anonymous tip out to the cops."

"Alright, you don't have to threaten me. I want the stuff no matter what," said Jones. "Just promise me you'll leave my boy out of this."

Two hours later, Jake watched from his tree cover as Chesterton Jones maneuvered his big cream-colored Cadillac Escalade down the drive to the Lodge, backing into some palmettos for cover. Whistling softly, Jake got his attention. Cautious, the big man looked around before approaching.

"Why'd you bring my boy into this, Collins?" said Jones without a greeting. Out of the air-conditioned Caddy, he was already sweating profusely. His eyes bulged when he saw the artifacts on the hood of the car, and forgot about his son and the heat, in his lust for what he saw. "Damnation! This is some good stuff—some of the best I've ever seen. I'd have bought it from you anyway—you know that. Ah, where'd you find it?"

"It's a secret," Jake said, his mouth curving into a smile that failed to reach his eyes. "You don't think I'm gonna tell you, of all people, where I dig, do you?"

His eyes glued to the artwork in an act of obeisance, the big man reached out to touch one of the pots. Collins saw it, and quickly moved between him and the collection. Chesterton sighed as he lowered the expensive safari hat on his brow, and pulled out the wad of hundred-dollar bills he carried to pay for transactions such as this.

Payment made and counted, Jake asked casually, "So, what's going on with that Hathaway bitch? She ever get out of the hospital?"

Chesterton flushed deep red at the question, "Not only is she 'out', she's blocked my nomination to the North Florida Wild Lands Restoration board. My company is pissed as all hell over it, but the board members, even Riggins can't overrule her in something like that. The plan was to help them go bankrupt then do a hostile takeover before they got their non-profit status. I was hoping you'd have finished her off by now. It may be more risk than you're willing to take, but we'd feather your nest quite well if you'd consider taking her out on our behalf."

Thinking of the snakes back in Steinhatchee and figuring he was with a human version of one, Jake kicked the sand at his feet and responded, "Not only would I consider it, I would take great pleasure in helping that nosy old biddy into the next world. How much you payin'?"

Looking away from the man in front of him, Jones stared up at the darkening sky. "How about a down payment of $50,000, and $50,000 on completion of the deed?" he said.

Jake whistled, "Man, y'all are serious about this, ain't you? It's a deal! Now, let me see the green." Stuffing the money into his pockets, he helped carry the artifacts to the Caddy, then strutted into the woods with fat pockets and disappeared, calling out in a disembodied voice, "I'll be in touch. Don't try to find me, 'cause if you do, I'll let it be known you were seen at the *White's Only Club* in Perry!"

The Caddy lurched towards him then turned, breaks squealing in the sand. Waiting until Chesterton's brake lights were well out of sight before coming out of the scrub, Jake tried to think. For the moment, he had more money on his person than he had ever had in his life—easy money, the best kind, but it would all be for nothing if he didn't bag his quarry. For now, he needed to lay low in case Jones' forgot his promises or the Coast Guard got too close, but first, it was time to celebrate.

He entered the lodge's rustic dining room and feasted on fried shrimp, oysters, scallops, grouper, coleslaw, hush-puppies, and cheese grits, topping it off with authentic key-lime pie. Booking a room, he paid in cash and slept in comfort the night through with no dreams. Later that day he hitched a ride down to Ocala and lay low, picking up a job at Silver Springs cleaning glass-bottom boats. It was enough to keep him distracted for a while, and allowed him a curious kind of anonymity. Management cared little for *who* cleaned the boats—just that they were presentable for guests to enjoy each day. While news from Tallahassee was spotty and focused mostly on political issues, still, he heard snatches and knew he was definitely on the "Most Wanted" list." He smiled to himself and bided his time. By mid-November, he was back in southern Leon County, digging in Magnolia, and watching. It was time.

Chapter 31

When she was well enough and could climb the stairs without fainting, Matt and Bobbie Ann helped BJ move home to the river house with great reluctance. Knowing Jake Collins was still at large kept them all on alert, but BJ felt it was time to get on with her life. At first, she was listless, memories of the kidnapping following her everywhere she went, but there were also Sasha and Martha. Together, the animals were her constant companions, never leaving her alone for even a minute.

At night, she longed for Matt. In the long months of recuperation, they had fallen into a companionable routine and her defenses had gradually dropped again. He was more considerate than ever, but now that she was back in the river house on her own turf, she missed seeing him every day, missed his rough beard and warm arms in the morning. She wanted him, but didn't know how to make it happen. That she loved him completely was no longer in any doubt.

To keep her mind active and off Jake Collins' whereabouts, she kept up with the restoration efforts via email and the phone, going so far as to hold a board retreat at the river house in an effort to get to know the members better. She maintained the North Florida Wild Lands Restoration website herself, steadily building their donor list through phone calls, emails and letters. She got in touch with experts in the area, including one of her favorite professors from Florida State who had worked tirelessly to restore wiregrass into the region's sandy soil, and deepened her knowledge of the place with intense study.

One of her greatest pleasures was the harvesting of planted slash pines and burning the land in preparation for re-planting the once abundant long-leaf pines. She documented the entire process with a fund-raising book in mind, keeping herself occupied as she healed. That she still couldn't venture into the woods or onto the river was a great hindrance, as she found extensive exercise difficult to maintain and breathe at the same time. Frequently she stormed at Jake Collins, venting in the silent house then regretting it when the chest rattle set in, her voice hoarse from exertion. Both Sasha and Martha went into hiding during those times, making her feel guilty for the hatred she felt towards Collins. Her feelings for the man often boiled over, but she refused to live in fear of his return. Part of her *wanted* to engage him and get it over with, but when it happened again—as she knew it would, she intended to win.

While she had a rifle, and was already licensed and proficient at using one, BJ got a small gun to carry at all times. She practiced with the little firearm frequently, aiming at a target set up next to the sawdust pile Jake desecrated in search of the mysterious black metal box. Somehow, it felt good to shoot at the area where he had tramped down her flower garden, but as time went on, even those emotions relaxed. She no longer replayed the horrible nightmare every night, and turned her mental faculties to an intense review of Ben's books about the ecology of North Florida.

Meanwhile, her relationship with Matt deepened, and her comfort level grew to the point she hated to see him leave at night and looked forward to every visit. Bobbie Ann watched in approval from a distance, keeping silent unless asked.

Intimacy, when it came, was deeply poignant—a gentle give and take that stirred them both, and so different from the wild passion of their youth. Late one evening, they sat watching the sun go down, windows open to the sounds of the night—mullet jumping in the river, crickets and the lone coyote that roamed nearby.

BJ dropped her book and listened, a smile on her lips. Matt felt the stillness and looked up; her eyes were on him, a mysterious look on her face. Without thinking, he leaned over and kissed her. She responded to that kiss with intensity, and when he finally drew back, both knew it was time.

In what felt like a trance, they walked into the moonlit bedroom. They danced slowly before the moon goddess, disrobing one another in the sacred ritual of mating, bowing to passion long restrained. They would need it for what was soon to come.

Chapter 32

BJ drove into Tallahassee with Matt, who was also on the board, for her first Wild Lands Restoration Trust meeting since the attack. The board members welcomed her warmly. She knew most of them from her time as Ben's intern, then her first meetings with the board when she moved back to Florida. One new member, Royce Riggins, formerly with the New Florida Bank, she had not met. She had reviewed his resume with the others, but she was unprepared for the feeling of disquiet she experienced on meeting him in person. Tall with white hair and fair skin that reddened easily, he held her hand just a fraction longer than was necessary. His gray eyes lingered on hers until she grew uncomfortable, turning away from him to greet other members of the board. Matt saw it, and moved to her side, his hand on her elbow. She did not resist the gesture, grateful for his support.

Rafe Alford, as chair, greeted her warmly and called the meeting to order and BJ began with her presentation. She was in the middle of expressing her desire to proceed with the Goose Pasture project, when Riggins' voice interrupted, startling the other members around the table.

"I understand you want to go in and put things to right at the Goose Pasture, especially in view of your recent escapade down there with Jake Collins," a slight sneer in his voice. While alarmed at his crude comment, Alford allowed him to continue, in order to see where it would lead. "Since you haven't been here in a quite some time . . . don't you

145

think you should hear about what we're already working on? Like the wire grass project?"

Rafe Alford, enraged by the man's insensitivity, started to call Riggins down, but when BJ ignored the tone and asked to hear his concerns, Alford—hackles still raised, backed off.

By the time Riggins finished, BJ found her project stalled, because everything was in stasis. She sensed Riggins' satisfaction as he sauntered out with a cool nod in her direction.

"What's going on with him, Rafe?" she asked Alford.

Alford thought for a moment before answering her. "Well, I'll tell you what I think, and you can make up your own mind. When I sent the letter telling the board about your inheritance, Riggins—who came on the board just before Ben died, was the only one who protested it. He said you were too *'green,'* and untried for the scope of the work, and that your appointment was a kind of nepotism. I explained to him that the whole project was Ben's dream, and he could leave his money and land to anyone he wanted. The board directs the projects now and controls the money held in trust for it, but the land continues under your direction until your demise. Riggins didn't like it then, and apparently still doesn't, and I really don't know why. I have my suspicions but they are just that—suspicious notions."

At the next meeting, BJ was careful to cultivate a courteous friendship with Riggins, even agreeing to meet him and Jim Haskins for coffee downtown in Tallahassee. Haskins told them Florida Wildlife officers had discovered two men at the old Wakulla Beach hotel the night before. "The Wildlife folks said they hadn't done any damage," he told them. "At first it appeared they were just hanging out for the privacy, which isn't unusual due to the area's isolation. When the officers flashed their lights at them, one ran off into the woods and got away. The one they caught is Ches Jones' son."

At BJ's exclamation and Riggins' obvious concern, he continued with a grin, "Yep, it was the boy again. Chip, I think they call him… but this time he was butt naked—and makin' it with the other man, too

146

stoned to run far. The boy said he didn't know the man he was with.…
The clincher is that he was in possession of illegal drugs, a shit-load of
cash—excuse me, BJ, and an unusual Apalachee artifact—all of it found
in the front seat of his daddy's big, cream-colored Caddy Escalade. He's
sittin' out at the City jail right now."

Turning to Riggins, he added, "I believe you are real close to
Chesterton Jones, and the boy's your godson. What have you got to say
to that?"

Riggin's neck turned red and enveloped his face all the way to
the scalp, causing his silky mane of white hair to glow pink.

"What do you mean telling *me* it was Ches' son?" he said; spit
flying out of his mouth. "We've known one another most of our lives,
and that boy *is* my godson, but I didn't raise him and I'm not responsible
for his actions!"

"I guess this means you didn't read the Tallahassee Democrat this
morning. I'm glad BJ kept Chesterton Jones off the board. It looks awful
bad when one of our board members makes the morning paper, don't
you think?" said Haskins with a glance to BJ.

BJ nodded, saying nothing, and simply watched the interplay
between the two men.

Angry, Riggins pushed his chair back and stomped out of the
room, cell phone in hand. BJ could see him standing in the hall through
the open door, and saw the furtive glances he threw at their table as he
spoke.

Riggins paid his bill and left, leaving BJ and Haskins to wonder
what was really going on. Later that day, they learned from Rafe Alford
that the boy was out on bail, but that Alford had resigned from the case
citing conflict of interest.

147

Chapter 33

At first, Jake chuckled when he read about the escapade in the paper. They *were* having sex on the beach, and it wasn't the first time, but the thing nobody knew was the Jones' boy was also negotiating for another ivory fore-shaft from the unidentified male on behalf of his father, Chesterson Jones, and his godfather, Royce Riggins.

Bisexual, Jake enjoyed playing with the boy, sensing his homosexual leanings not long after their first meeting, but now he regretted the dalliance. The Jones brat was spoiled and probably scared silly; he would spill everything he knew even if his daddy paid for the best lawyer money could buy. Cautious, he hung out for two days in the bog jungle, eating swamp cabbage and drinking brackish water to avoid discovery. Finally, filled with morbid curiosity, he went down to the sinkhole where he pushed BJ over the edge, then on to the charred remains of the yellow trailer. The complete destruction of the trailer at his hand gave him some satisfaction, but it angered him that BJ lived still. He found a floating fish camp on the river not far from the ruins of his old place, moved in and laid low, planning the mode of attack. It was time to do the arrogant old biddy in, then to clear out for good. It made him angry just to think about BJ Hathaway. Her intrusion cost him what he considered his inheritance, and now he was in trouble with Jones and Riggins, too, unless he killed her very soon. It was time to make his move.

He sat on a stump in the swamp counting money for a while, swatting yellow flies and thinking about his nemesis, BJ Hathaway. It amused him to eliminate the source of his troubles for cold hard cash—there was a raw sense of justice in it to his way of thinking.

To get a sense of BJ's movements, he made his way down to the river house in the guise of a fisherman every day. Jake knew she had that cursed hound dog, a deputy passed by frequently, and it seemed like either Bobbie Ann Rice or Matt Walker and his mangy mutt were there all the time. On occasion, watching from the water, he saw her sitting with friends in the breezeway under the house with the ceiling fan whirring above them in the evening. *He gritted his teeth and waited.*

* * *

At times, when BJ sat on the deck or in the breezeway, the hair on the back of her neck rose uncomfortably. She wondered if life would ever feel normal again, or if the need to watch her back would always be there. There was no reason to think Jake Collins was watching her, but often she wondered if he was. No word of him had reached her for over a year, but thoughts of him stayed close. There were even times she considered going back to New Mexico, but that would mean running away. She did not to want live her life in fear of the man, but she was doing just that.

* * *

One afternoon, Jake's patience paid off when he heard the cop car take off, sirens screaming. He grinned, knowing Walker's truck was gone, and Bobbie Ann was at her place. He moved in closer.

BJ was restless. Over a year since the rescue, she was essentially recovered, anxious to get on with her life. She continued to use a burnt bamboo walking stick for stairs or walking the trails near the house with friends. There was satisfaction in what she was doing now. Work was progressing on the Goose Pasture project, which had finally gotten off the ground, and controls were in place to protect Wakulla Beach from development and looting, but still, she was filled with a strange sort of angst. She felt eyes on her all the time even when she knew none were there—maybe she was losing her mind. She needed to get out of the house, suddenly feeling claustrophobic.

149

When she heard the patrol car leave, its departure seemed to set her free. Against her better judgment, she decided to take her first solo walk around Taylor's Run. It had been some time since she had the energy for much exercise, but the day was crisp and beautiful as only North Florida can be in the winter, and she had to get into it. She pulled on a flannel shirt, grabbed Ben's old felt hat, leashed Sasha, and took off.

It felt good to be outside and alone for once. The air was bracing, and she felt energized by it.

Jake watched patiently as BJ disappeared up the track towards the road. When she and the dog were out of sight, he casually made his way up the back steps and entered the house as he had always done. He was surprised to see how light and clean it was now. Her contributions were comfortable furniture, more bookcases and southwestern rugs strewn on the floor.

There was coffee in the pot, so he casually poured himself a cup and settled down to wait for his quarry in the quiet house. Didn't she know he'd come back eventually? She deserved to die for her stupidity.

Chapter 34

Jake heard the hound bay as it strained to pull toward the trail he had used to walk up from the water, and then heard BJ laugh and call it back to her side. He grinned at the innocent concern in her voice, thinking if she only knew who was in her house, she would be running away, not walking into what he planned for her.

They turned towards the house and began the trek up the path. Sasha still showed signs that something was wrong, but everything looked just as it had when BJ left it minutes before. Perhaps an opossum had crossed the trail—that would be enough to set Sasha off, to be sure. Oblivious to the real danger just ahead, she moved forward.

Sasha refused to heel. Nose to the ground she growled, tail tucked under, and pulled at the leash, almost dragging BJ in her haste to follow the scent. BJ fingered the little gun in her pocket— she kept it with her always—that and her phone. Some latent instinct made her press the speed-dial to both Matt and the sheriff; sending them an ICE text for backup, she held onto the dog and struggled up the stairs.

Martha was in hiding as usual—since Sasha's arrival she had taken to staying in BJ's room most of the time, and was probably hiding under the bed waiting to be coaxed out. Sasha continued to growl, and slowly, keeping her grip on Sasha's collar, she walked through the silent house, searching for signs of intrusion.

* * *

Sasha's cold nose bumped her leg, a low threatening growl deep in her throat. BJ knew then that something was very wrong in the next room. The hound strained against the collar BJ still held, the ridgeline on her back stiff.

"Is somebody here?" BJ whispered, breaking out in a cold sweat. Her hand went to the gun in her pants pocket. She gripped the pearl-handle, ready to defend herself. When she heard the dreaded voice, her hand froze.

"Well, lookie here, ain't you something sittin' purdy on this here piece of property that was my granddaddy's land. You sleep with ole' Ben so's you could have it?"

The exaggerated drawl that was more put-on southern than real, was one she expected to hear again but not now, not here again in her own house, and especially not when she was alone. She had grown careless and might not live to regret it.

There, sitting in Ben's rocking chair with a cup of her coffee in his hand, was Jake Collins.

Suddenly, Sasha jerked away from her and leaped at the man, snarling. Jake, who had been watching the dog, was ready, and kicked it hard in the head. The dog collapsed at his feet and lay still. BJ ran to it and dropped to her knees, cradling the bleeding head in her lap.

With a leering grin, Collins grabbed her by the hair, yanked her to her feet and dragged her to the bed. He threw her down hard. It hurt— her body, though technically healed, still held memories from the sinkhole, and Jake's rough treatment brought them back in painful waves. The bed felt like concrete when she hit it, knocking the breath out of her lungs.

In pain, afraid to breathe but gasping for air, she lay still, watching the dreaded face looming over her. Jake glared down at her, his face rock hard with anger, lips drawn back over bad teeth in a sneer. She tried to turn away, but he grabbed her face in a painful grip and forced her to look at him.

152

"Now I'm gonna do what I wanted to do back the night you jilted me at the prom. I bet you thought I forgot about that, didn't you—you old biddy, but I didn't," he said, continuing to rant. "Ole' Jake, he don't never forget a slight, especially from a stuck-up bitch like you. I should 'a done it a 'fore I pushed you into the sinkhole. You done took my land away from me, and everything else that should be mine, and I ain't gonna let you get away with it. You always did think you was too good for the rest of us. Well, that ain't so."

He tore at her clothes with savage violence, ripping them off in his anger. She fought back, struggling to get the gun from her jeans pocket, but he was too strong. She found herself naked and flat on her back, frantically trying to escape. She tried to cover herself and roll off the bed when he unzipped his pants, but he held her with his legs—she couldn't move. Closing her eyes, she struggled, still unwilling to believe what was happening, until she felt her legs brutally forced apart. She found herself staring in horror at the specter of Jake Collins about to enter her deepest self when he froze. His protruding member wilted as he found himself violently dragged away from her, and slammed against the wall.

Breathing hard, BJ dropped off the bed on the other side, scrambling to cover herself with the spread. She reached for her jeans, and found the gun. Quickly, she pulled it out, released the safety and cocked it, only to find Matt and Chi between her and Collins.

Matt moved quickly, savagely penning Jake to the wall. He got in one good hit, grabbing Collins by the throat as he sank, when Randal Crum's voice cut through the air: "Don't do it, Walker. He ain't worth it. Let me take him in."

Walker relaxed his grip on Collins' throat just enough for the man to make a move. With energy born of desperation and fear, Collins slid from his grasp, evading both Walker and Crum, and raced for the stairs. Chi, Collins' nemesis, topped him before he made it to the door.

Babbling—the whites of his eyes showing how great was his fear, Jake pleaded with Walker to call the dog off, then, without warning, slid out of the open French doors on the run. BJ stopped him with one shot. Matt always swore he felt the bullet whiz past before it entered Jake Collins' left shoulder, just above the heart, catching him as he jumped over the deck railing. He fell to the ground bleeding, and sobbing in pain with one leg bent backwards. Chi, who had raced down the stairs, lunged at him, snarling and snapping.

"My God, but that was a good shot!" said the sheriff to BJ, with admiration in his voice. Pointing his gun at Jake, who was crying like a baby and begging to be rescued from Chi, Crum called down to his deputy, "Rusty, tell the First Responders to get up here, and then you and Jimbo cuff that man and get him out of here real quick before I let that dog loose on him."

Matt wrapped BJ in the bed quilt and lifted her in his arms. Avoiding eye contact, she pressed her face into his neck as hot tears soaked them both. They were standing like that when BJ heard whimpering. It was Sasha, lying in a pool of blood.

"No, no!" she cried. "Sasha!"

The dog was breathing, but just barely, when the Sheriff lifted her up and ran down the stairs to the ambulance. "Here, see to this dog before you do him," he said, nodding at the blubbering Jake. "It's the dog from the sinkhole!"

Another ambulance arrived soon after to attend to Jake Collins, but not before Sasha left in the first ambulance, sirens blaring, for surgery at the animal hospital in Crawfordville.

Chapter 35

Jake transferred from the hospital to the jail after sufficiently recovering from his wounds. He was held there without bond awaiting his day in court. He waited for the trial to begin, and did it in isolation due to threats made against him by some of the inmates. Still, he exhibited no remorse, showing a secretive, almost leering half-smile when anyone appeared at the tiny window of his cell. Numerous members of the community set up a watch around the jail; sitting in dead silence day and night, they were like dread specters waiting for carrion. In reality, the community determined Jake Collins would not escape, and stood guard until the expedited case went before Judge Robert M. Whaley.

The case then went to Grand Jury and in record time, their recommendation went to the judge. On the day of sentencing, it seemed as though most of Wakulla *and* southern Leon County filled the Federal Courthouse in Tallahassee to maximum capacity. When Jake walked in, escorted by several armed guards, he was dressed in prison-orange, heavily shackled, his dirty blond hair long, beard scraggly, but on his face was that same disconcerting half-smile. The room went quiet when he approached the bench to be sworn-in.

At first, it seemed some of Jake's former cockiness was gone. Then, just as he took his seat, he turned around, scanned the room and found BJ. Staring straight into her eyes, he grinned and winked. Matt saw it and heard her gasp. He took her hand quickly as a cloud of murmuring rose in the courtroom and the judge slammed his gavel down hard.

At the reading of Jake's crimes, bile rose in BJ's gut, she almost strangled in the gag reflex. Her kidnapping, Robin's body in the thick, black bag, the explosion and fire, the sinkhole and finally, the near rape loomed large before her.

Fighting nausea, and drenched with perspiration in the chill courtroom, BJ longed to escape, but she would not give Jake that satisfaction. Instead, she looked back at him, steeling herself against his thoughts, sending some of her own across the room like swords across the expanse. It was, however, difficult to sit there and have the past replayed in public before friends and strangers. She felt their stares, and in most cases, sympathy, but also felt anger swelling in her chest. When the defense attorney began with excuses for Jake's behavior, she saw red and knew fury. How could anyone possibly excuse what that man had done?

As the day dragged on, Jake's shoulders began to droop, and the little smile faded. Chesterton Jones, his son Chip, and Royce Riggins, gave testimony about their dealings with him, telling the underbelly of the story, and their part in it (but not all.) Those disclosures from such prominent executives shocked everyone in the courtroom and ruined all three for life. Finally, there was no place for Jake to find cover—the gruesome story was out in the open, drawing attention from all over the nation. By the time the case went to the jury, and he was led out of the courtroom, his swagger was gone; it appeared Jake Collins was finally afraid.

* * *

The jury re-entered five and one half hours later. This time, Jake kept his eyes lowered, refusing to look up. The jury-foreman read the verdict: guilty as charged. The judge passed the sentence—life in prison with no parole.

BJ felt the tension in her shoulders release—how could something that had commandeered so much of her life be over so

156

quickly? How could she resume something akin to a normal life? Bobbie Ann squeezed her hand, but she barely felt it. Matt put his arm around her shoulders, but she felt numb and cold and wanted only to escape from them all. Sheriff Crum led them from the courthouse past eager reporters jostling one another for a place near her. Fortunately, her old friend, Andrea Bratton, the Democrat's investigative reporter was there, and after speaking briefly to the press in passing, BJ granted an exclusive interview to her. They met later over coffee at BJ's place, where Andrea was mercifully to the point. Few knew the story better than she did, having followed it from the very beginning.

Chapter 36

Finding in the river house constant reminders of her most recent encounter with Jake, BJ withdrew into herself, finding solace at Bobbie Ann's place this time. Too many things had happened, tampering with the fragile relationship she and Matt enjoyed; she withdrew from him too.

Puzzled, but knowing BJ too well to interfere, Matt made himself available, but he was in unfamiliar territory. Never had he been close to anyone who had survived so many disasters in such a short span of time, nor had he been with a woman who had come so close to rape. His hatred for Jake Collins mounted to obsession. Nursing his own private hurts with work, he delved into the woods of Magnolia to salvage what Jake had despoiled. A delegation of the First People, descendants of the Miccosukee and Apalachee Indians worked with him to recover and repair the damage wrecked on the ancient site. Nothing salvaged his heart.

* * *

Just a week after Jake's sentencing, BJ abruptly called a stunned Matt to tell him she was leaving for New Mexico and had no idea when she would return. She closed the river house, leaving with Martha and Sasha without looking back. Taking her things out of storage in Santa Fe, she rented a small apartment and resumed study of the Pueblo culture with an almost rabid intensity. For the most part, beyond a cursory

158

explanation, she avoided her old friends and their need to know everything about the craziness back in Florida. Concerned, they watched from a distance, ready should she need them, but she seldom called. Preferring to be alone, BJ spent hours on end in the hot, dry desert so drastically different from Florida, searching for traces of the ancient culture, trying to find the peace that eluded her.

She often thought of Ben. Had he known Jake's potential for true harm, he might never have set up the path they inevitably followed. She went back over everything she did from the time of Ben's death and the journey back to Florida, trying to make sense of it, but there was no good reason for what happened. She couldn't escape a sense of misplaced personal responsibility, and finally accepted the necessity for therapy. After some months of gut-wrenching work, she took the slow path to healing, learning to reframe events and to appreciate the time taken in the wilderness to complete her research.

Some months into BJ's sojourn in New Mexico, Sheriff Randall Crum called. "BJ, that you?" he said. "Listen to me, you'd better set yourself down for this. Jake Collins is dead. Turns out the other inmates hated his guts and were out to get him. They don't think it was suicide from the way it was done—somebody cut him up bad. He bled to death, alone in his cell last night."

Numb, BJ listened to the tale without responding. Sasha put her head in BJ's lap but the hand that normally caressed her lay still.

"BJ, did you hear what I just said?" Crum said, his voice excited, "Listen to me, BJ. He's gone. Dead. You ain't never gonna' have to worry about him no more. You hear me?" Finally, she responded, telling him in a whisper, "Thanks for telling me Randall, let me call you later, okay? I've got to let this sink in before I can talk."

"Well, alright. I just wanted you to be the first to know," he said, deflated by her lack of response.

Perversely, and without further comment beyond answering cursory questions about Jake's death, BJ went back to her work on the Pueblos. Eventually accumulating enough material to finish her book, she closed the Santa Fe apartment, and then went home to face her demons in Florida without telling anyone she was coming. Timing was everything: she needed to face the house on the river alone. Matt was out of the country on an expedition, Bobbie Ann was caring for a patient in her new role as a volunteer with Big Bend Hospice, so she had the river and the big house to herself. Climbing those steps again, she half-expected Ben to call out, or Jake to be waiting in the bedroom, but all was quiet on the river. Sasha bounded in as though she had never been away while Martha raced to her special spot under the bed. Everything was as it should be, down to the worn boots on the mat by the door, Ben's old hat on its hook, and the flannel shirt hanging on its straight-backed chair. All was clean, and her personal collections were back where they should be thanks to Matt and Bobbie Ann. She was home.

Suddenly glad to be there, BJ grabbed the leash and called Sasha. Without unpacking, she locked up and went down to the dock to check on the Jon boat. Again, all was as it should be, down to the raucous welcome from the eagles high above. When the little motor sprang to life at her touch, she knew this was the right thing to do. She would visit the site of her near demise.

She found the yellowed vegetation that still marred Blackwater Creek, letting the boat take her through the dark tunnel of trees. She fought nausea all the way, but it was something she had to do. The swampy wilderness was recovering, but still, scars from Jake's occupation were there. When she found the cans clustered around the cypress knees, she knew the time had come to confront her pain.

Tying the boat off, she clamored around the knotty growths in the water, skirting a drowsy water moccasin and scattering minnows in her path. She kept on until she reached the charred remains of the trailer that was Robin's funeral pyre. She kept Sasha at her side, the dog's familiar presence reassuring in the swamp with its miasma of foul smells and decaying memories.

Thankfully, although she felt deep remorse for Robin, there was now little of Jake in the swamp but residual damage. For the first time

160

since the trial, his face was blurry, the quirky, evil grin gone from her mind, the sound of his voice distant.

Fascinated by the swamp's smoky peat bog, still simmering from the fire, BJ saw that nature, in fact, *was* fast restoring herself—vines grew over the remains of the trailer, and nearby she felt the presence she detected on that fateful day she spent there. Walking further into the forest, following the mystical call she had heard before, and one that seemed to envelop her entire being, she found the source—the big tree Ben showed her so many years before. The ancient cypress was scarred by the fire as were all the trees nearby, and its base was scratched, the stringy bark hanging in tatters. Miraculously, it was alive. At its base was a huge mussel shell, probably left by a bear, and she sat down against the tree with the mollusk in her hands, Sasha's weight pressed against her thigh. It seemed as though the pain that had left her emotionally crippled for months began to drain into the rich soil at her feet. Stump settin,' a wise woman named Awiakta, once called it. When she left the ancient tree, it was with a restored sense of mission for herself—there was much to do here, and now, she had the time and the tools to accomplish the tasks that lay ahead.

She felt alive on the trip back to the river house—alive, strong and determined. Her heart lifted when she heard again the cry of the eagles—welcome to an old friend.

* * *

One chilly night in November, she and Sasha were out for their evening walk, when she felt an urge to turn towards Matt's place that would not be denied. How she had missed him, but she couldn't forget their last encounter with Jake. Because of those horrific memories, she kept Matt at a distance. He seemed to understand most of the time, giving her the space she needed, but there was often deep sadness in his eyes that hurt her to the quick. Now, however, both woman and dog as one walked down the path to his cabin instead of the river house. Seeing a fire flickering in the hearth through the window, and his feet on the hassock, she let herself in. Chi responded to her signal and kept quiet, his tail slowly wagging a welcome.

161

She walked into the room, wondering if the man sleeping by the fire would even care that she was there. Watching him under lowered lids, BJ caressed the tussled hair in her mind, hair that had gone from iron gray to white in the past year, hair that she loved so much. She imagined his touch—gifted hands roughened by hard outdoor work, on her body, and felt a thrill at the memory of when he touched her in the past; a time when her own wild hair was jet black, her skin smooth and free of the wrinkles and scars it now bore. More than anything, she wanted to feel free to sit next to him, to settle her body close to his and feel his arms wrap around her.

At last, awareness seeped through sleep, and when he looked up, Matt saw a woman past her prime in some ways, but one filled with the wisdom of the moment. The friend and partner he knew loved him. Chi and Sasha, sitting close to one another by the hearth, looked from one to the other and settled their heads on steady paws, waiting to see what would happen to their people.

BJ stood still, watching Matt, wondering what to do next. He smiled then, and her heart leapt when she saw fire spark in those green eyes staring straight into hers. He uncrossed his legs and opened his arms and she went to him without speaking, not taking her eyes off his. She knew what she wanted, and moved into him and buried her face in the hollow between his neck and shoulder. She felt the kiss on top of her head just where she had known it would be. When he lifted her chin and kissed her lips, everything fell into place and she wondered why it had taken them so long to get to this most natural of places—a man and a woman who loved one another, and wanted nothing more than to be together, for as long as there was time.

Saundra Gerrell Kelley

Saundra was born in Tallahassee, the capital of Florida. She says, "I am a genuine Florida Cracker - a descendent of sturdy women and men who farmed their way south from North Carolina in the early 1800s. I am a graduate of Florida State University with a BS in Social Science, and earned an MA in Education/Storytelling from East Tennessee State University. My work is deeply influenced by a love and reverence for the natural world and environmental issues and my love of story."

Saundra currently lives in Tennessee. She works as a professional storyteller and spends much of her time writing. McFarland Publishers released, <u>Southern Appalachian Storytellers: Interviews with Sixteen Keepers of the Oral Tradition</u>, in 2011. This is her debut novel.

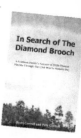

CPSIA information can be obtained at www.ICGtesting.com
Printed in the USA
LVOW13s0121260314

378876LV00001B/142/P